CHARLIE

CHARLIE

Father, widower, recovering commando

Finn Óg

Columbus, Ohio

Charlie

Published by Gatekeeper Press
3971 Hoover Rd. Suite 77
Columbus, OH 43123-2839
www.GatekeeperPress.com

ISBN: 9781619847293
eISBN: 9781619847309

Printed in the United States of America

"One crowded hour of glorious life,
is worth an age without a name."

For Lachlan, never forgotten.

One Zero

I knew that they'd come for me. Deep down. It was inevitable really, despite my precautions. I think I might have been waiting for it. Perhaps even willing it.

Guilt is unfathomable. I felt a lot of guilt. About how I'd chosen to earn a living. About the risks I was taking. About not having been there, when I was truly needed. I was guilty of pursuing vengeance, satisfaction, and purpose. I was guilty of grief.

As soon as I woke that night, I knew I hadn't been clever enough. I had planned, certainly, but they'd found us. My initial thought was that I had underestimated them. In actual fact, I had misidentified them.

*****

I really had tried to stick to what I knew, when I got home. The problem was what I knew. I knew boat work, so that was where I began. But that notion slipped away, like the ashes I'd shaken into a gentle sea breeze. My principle concern was Isla, our daughter. Well, my daughter. For three days, she had suffered without me, as the Corps thrashed around to get me replaced and repatriated from Bastion. She was with my folks, which was as good as it could possibly have been, but nothing makes up for a parent, and she had only one left. I knew she would be terrified of losing another, and so I knew too, that I would never wear webbing again.

The mind, well mine at least, tends to turn to the practical as a protection measure, an escape from emotion. For three days, I kept the grief at bay, slowly working through what I would do, and how I would do it. Others said I was in shock. I wasn't. Perhaps because of my training, perhaps because of my nature, I just worked towards securing a way forward for us.

The end game was to wrap Isla in love, to assure her that nobody could harm her, or me, and that she was safe. I knew how obsessed she could become with little things. I recall being similar myself, when I was so small. Because of what had happened to her mum, she would be terrified of every noise at the house, every opening of the front door, every coming and going. The solution presented itself in a straightforward fashion; we wouldn't live in a house. But then the problems crowded in, as the head-banging judder of the transport flight rattled me all the way home. Who would buy a house like ours, given what had happened there?

Admittedly, there was a part of me that enjoyed the musings of revenge. I had been equipped with the necessary skills, and I would use them. I tried again and again not to focus on such urges, but my planning was frequently overcome by them. In between such blistering impulses, I carved out a future for my daughter and I.

Much revolved around her nature. She deserved a beautiful life, to be sheltered from the type of conflict that had brought her mother and I together. I suspected that one day, Isla would follow in her mother's footsteps – a frightening prospect. Her Mam and I had met amid horror, as she worked to preserve life, and I to extinguish it. Isla had inherited her kindness. I could see it in every subtle gesture she made. She was programmed to be as gentle, as I was built for brutality. Admittedly her mother had managed to coax some dormant empathy from deep within me, but keeping that at the surface was a constant challenge.

*****

Amid the slapping and tapping of rigging and waves, a single creak seemed out of place. It was possible that an army of otters had clambered aboard again, and that I had been roused by their tails hammering the deck. But I'd been around some tight corners in the preceding months, and it just didn't feel like that.

A barely perceptible heave of the hull to port confirmed it; there was someone above me. I stood silent, waiting for the next step to betray the visitor's position. The aluminium hull was solid, but only a ballerina would have the grace and balance to move undetected, just a few inches over my head.

The days of sweat and screaming with Yank SWAT teams told me to draw the intruder below deck, to let the confined-combat training kick in, but I had more to protect that night than a nuclear submarine.   I opted for the rear hatch. The cover lifted silently. My emergence was masked by the rubber dinghy I'd slung on deck before dinner. I was half in, half out of the boat. I felt the same exposure my pals must have endured in the desert, gunning out the roof of our amphibious Vikings vehicles, as I'd gazed at their bootlaces below. I lifted myself up. And that's when the darkness returned.

I'd never felt fear like that. When I came around, the alarm hit me instantly. Where was Isla? I jolted my face upwards from the deck of our cutter. My cheek had been glued to the teak by my own slabber. Again, the thought crossed my mind, where was my daughter? What the hell had happened?

I rounded on myself. Instinct I suppose. What was behind me? Had I been hit? How long had I been out?

I saw the hulk of a man lying a few feet away, belly-up, motionless. I rolled over the coach roof, landed on his chest, and struck him hard, but he was plainly gone. His eyes betrayed his method of departure. Who the hell was he?

I tore below deck, through the main cabin, and wrenched open the bunk door. There lay Isla, sound asleep, her little arm hanging from under the covers. I crouched beside her and hugged her tight. Then I paused, muttering my thanks. Over and over. She could sleep through a gale, my wee five-year-old.

"Hallo, Daddy," she muttered, not even half awake, and rolled back into the heat. As she turned away from me, I noticed the blood on my thumbs.

I returned to the deck, and scoured the surrounding sea. Nothing. I walked around the boat, eyes trained towards the water line, looking for a kayak, or dinghy. Still, nothing. Realising that time was short, I skipped below and fired up the radar. It took an interminable time to acquire its position and begin sweeping. Nothing. Absolutely nothing.

I returned to the dead man on deck. I tried to re-boot my memory as I searched him.

We were anchored miles from land. If he had been delivered by boat, surely I would have seen it escape? Surely the radar would have picked it up?

But there was no dinghy, he had no identification, and worst of all, he was dry.

Two

It was her smile that had disarmed me, as I squelched up a beach in Gaza. Thankfulness shone out of her.

The call had come as we were training at our home port in Poole, in the south of England. From there we'd been flown to Faslane Naval Base in Scotland, a place with which we were all familiar. We'd gathered our kit together, been briefed, and boarded a submarine. It had dived mid-Med, and one hundred nautical miles off the shore of Egypt, we were launched to the surface. In the swell, we inflated the boat, ripped the outboard engine from its waterproof bag, and motored further east. The risk increased as we got closer to Israeli territorial waters. The boat had to meander at a snail's pace to avoid radar interest. Ten miles from the coast we attached our fins over lightweight boots, and returned to the sea. The coxswain, a Marine attached to our SBS unit, turned tail, and left four of us to kick ashore. Then it all started to go tits up.

Two miles from the sand, and on top of a rolling sea, we watched as rockets, presumably from an Israeli helicopter gunship, lit the night sky. I knew instinctively that they'd struck where we had intended to land, and that our chances of success were narrowing with each explosion. Because of the nature of our operation, we had virtually no comms. Israeli action so close to the coast meant that our commanding officer would not be able to send an assault craft to collect us. The search would take too long, and the Israelis would probably spot the boat, sparking a diplomatic inquiry, and a shit-fight with an ally. So we swam, and beached in hell.

Two of my team fanned right, the other left, as I made my way up the beach, tired and restricted by my wet kit. The night was black, as we had predicted, and we were wary of any impact the gunship attack might have had. We had not expected to find it so quickly. I was nearly on top of them before I realized what was happening. I stood stock still as another rocket flash lit the sky to my left, and betrayed the bodies before me. One appeared to be crouched over another, as it lay prostate on the sand. There was a moment before the darkness was restored, when a face turned towards me.

I clutched my knife, ready to remove the obstacle if necessary. My intentions were subverted though, when I heard her speak. "Who's there? For the love of God will ye not help me?"

I had been away from home for a very long time. In my early twenties, I'd taken a train with its own special stop to Devon. Thereafter I'd only returned to Ireland for holidays. Now, on a beach in the Middle-East, in the middle of the night, in the middle of a war, I was being asked for help by an Irishwoman. Her voice stripped me of all my sensibilities. I was supposed to lead the operation, to ignore all else and get the job done. Against all reason, I took my LED light from my belt, and shone it in her face.

That smile. In the midst of deepest misery, that's what caught me. It was a smile of hope, of faith. I hesitated longer than I should have on her beautiful face, and then panned the torch down. Her arms, to the elbows, were smothered in blood. The child at her knees was labouring for air, and my decision was made. The med pack in my kit was unrolled, and without a word I went to work, packing what was plainly a catastrophic bleed. I applied a tourniquet to the boy's upper leg, knowing that with it, he would lose his limb-without it, he would lose his life.

I refused to speak to the woman for as long as I was able, but the compulsion, as I finished, overwhelmed me. She asked me a few questions-I responded with silence. She must have sensed that I was not there for good reason, and so she, too, fell silent. As I packed up to go, she put her arms around me, and hugged me hard.

"Thank you," she whispered.

''No hassle," I replied, and I felt the shock shudder through her. Even with just two words, my accent is indisputable. She pulled back and although the white light had burned my night vision, I could sense her staring at me. Just then my team crawled up from behind, and swearing like the sailors they were, made clear their feelings on contact with the natives.

We extracted, my mates still cursing me. I knew though, somehow, that I'd see that woman again. I could not have imagined how, such was the simultaneous humanity and depravity of what our next meeting would bring.

*****

The fact that the intruder had not swum to our boat, really unnerved me. I'd chosen the anchorage for security, and privacy, so where was his accomplice? How had the dead man got on board, and where was his dinghy?

The closeness of the call summoned huge anger in me. What if he had killed me and left? What would my five-year-old have done? She would have been terrified. Called out for me, and like a good wee woman, she would eventually have put on her life jacket to come and find me. If I'd been forced overboard, she'd have been stranded. If I'd been killed, she'd have been orphaned.

I knew instantly where to dispose of the man. Isla and I had roamed an island not three days before which had a natural fall in the centre. From its marshy middle grew bracken and reeds, and the stagnant damp struck me, even then, as a perfect place to dispose of someone.

There is no easy way to transport a body. Even small people seem to weigh more when dead. This was something I had learned the hard way in Helmand, when a tough little Bootneck had bled out down my back. I wasn't prepared to take my daughter ashore with a body in the bilges. I feared that whoever had accompanied the intruder might arrive at the dock with a car full of cops. Isla had lost too much already, and separation from her daddy was not an option.

The answer came easily enough. I opened the deep cockpit locker and hauled out an enormous canvas bag, which contained the old mainsail. I lashed the sail soundly, toppled it back into the locker, and took the bag on deck. Tearing through the dead man's pockets proved fruitless, save for a packet of Drum tobacco, papers, and a wind resistant lighter. All of this was sealed in a small plastic sandwich bag, the type I occasionally sent my daughter to school with. At least it told me that he wasn't a man accustomed to being indoors.

His features lacked the Slavic, Eastern European angularity I'd half expected, given the way I had been occupying my time until then. His identity really was a mystery. His shoes were from Clark's, his jeans were from Next, and his t-shirt could have been from any high-street store. His belt was equally unremarkable, but for the fact that its circumference was tiny, in comparison to his shoulders. The base of his shoes had a bit of a tidemark, like he'd stepped in a puddle, but his feet had not been submerged. His back was moist, and his t-shirt stuck to it, and he looked fit enough, despite the fags.

I unfastened the main halyard shackle, looped it around his ankles, and winched him into the air, cursing the deep bloodstain he'd left on my timber. I took twenty feet of spare chain from a bucket in the bilge, and dropped it into the bottom of the canvas bag. Opening it at the neck, I drew it up and over the dangling corpse. It stopped just beyond his waist, and I could hear the man's head make contact with the chain. I had little time left before he stiffened beyond manipulation, so I let him down and folded his legs into the makeshift shroud. A rolling hitch with a loop secured the bag, and I used the main halyard again to lift the whole lot over the side, and into the water.

With the carcass secured about three feet below the hull, and the deck scrubbed as clear as I could make out in the half-light, I did two things I generally tried to avoid. I sat in the cockpit and rolled myself a dead man's cigarette, and worked backwards through my past. I had to fathom out who had planned to kill me, in light of what that would have meant for my daughter, now that her mum was gone.

*****

We'd been deployed, we thought, to protect a CHIS, a Covert Human Intelligence Source. I assumed it had been a request from the spooks, from Mi5 or 6, but we were never told. It seemed likely that some British agent inside an Irish republican paramilitary group, had found themselves at the centre of an arms swap with Palestinian militants. That agent must have passed the intelligence to his or her handlers, and that resulted in the four of us being sent to Gaza.

Back then I'd been a "volunteer" in a special unit, the SBS, or Special Boat Service. It's a bit like the SAS, except wetter. Our orders were to board an Irish ship, which was attempting to carry humanitarian aid into Gaza. The brief was to locate some dodgy old Semtex explosive, and extract with it. All I could work out was that the agent must have been worth keeping. Sending us into the middle of yet another upsurge in conflict between Israel and Hamas was no everyday call. What I couldn't work out was why British Intelligence had allowed the explosives to get on board the boat at all. If the Israelis ever found out that their allies, the Brits, had known that such a volatile substance was being shipped to its enemies, they'd be pretty pissed off. Anyway, it seemed fairly straightforward to us. Swim, land, locate the ship, take the stuff, extract. Of course, it didn't quite turn out that way.

Three

The night I met my wife, Shannon, rattled through my mind on the flight home from Afghanistan. I stared at the coffins lashed to the base of the C17's vacuous cargo bay, and thanked God that I hadn't known the poor unfortunates inside. It was almost laughable that some idiot at Kandahar Airfield thought it acceptable to place a bereaved Bootneck beside caskets. I imagine that was part of the grieving process, seeing death in everything, and tumbling through a life short-lived. It seemed important to remember our beginning together, now that we had our end. It was almost comforting to interrogate the detail about how we'd bonded over a terrible conceit.

I was ushered off the plane on the blind side. This prevented the relatives of the dead from seeing a bedraggled Marine emerge on foot, while their loved ones were carried, draped in the symbols of an unreciprocated loyalty. The dead Guardsmen had been woefully unprepared for Taliban tactics. I'd often seen them, marauding through the dusk, sky-lined and making noise, unconscious to the signs of mines and ambush.

From the Royal Air Force Base Lyneham, I was taken to the nearby military town of Wootton Bassett to buy some civilian clothes. English officers could travel freely in their kit, but I had to fly from Bristol to Belfast, where attitudes towards the UK military varied hugely.

It wasn't until I reached the civilian airport that a plan began to emerge. It has always been thus, my mind and heart darkening for long periods as I wallow in the horrors, but on every occasion, something has pointed me in the right direction. Thereafter, I have been able to work hard to get to that point in my imagination, where everything will be as good as it can be. Perhaps it's a form of internal therapy, where I listen to myself moan, and eventually shake it off.

Dressed in badly fitting clothes, I found myself starting to struggle with the imminent reunion with my daughter. My throat grew thick, and I could feel the backs of my eyes flounder in a rising tide. I knew that without a distraction, I might lose a fight I'd become accustomed to winning; that against any betrayal of emotion.

Mercifully, there was a vacant seat with a discarded newspaper upon it. I whipped it up before me and opened it at a random page. Breathing deeply and scanning hard, my eyes fell upon an advert for an auction to be held just outside Belfast. "No reserve!" it screamed, listing an aluminium sailing boat as the key lot. I had no idea at that stage what it was worth, or what it might sell for, but I knew that I would buy it. It felt as though my dead wife, in her gentle way, had drawn me towards it. From that point on I had a goal. The plan fell into place on the short hop home.

*****

In truth, my wife had become my life-guide years before. If I am re-programmed at all, it is down to her. She somehow instinctively knew that I needed to find a purpose for the skills instilled in me, and that a simple departure from life as a Commando would leave a void that would prove impossible to fill. When I saw her for the second time, she looked into my eyes so probingly that I felt she'd reached inside, and choked the indifference out of me.

Of course, there never should have been a second contact. We were not supposed to spend any significant time in Gaza at all, but the intensity of the assault unleashed by Israel on that dry, dusty, dismal strip of land disrupted our plans. The Palestinian group Hamas was in control in the area, politically and militarily, and had enormous support among the population. Using that cover, Hamas had decided, on the same bloody night we landed, to resume rocket attacks over the fence into Israel. The Israeli Defence Force reacted with its usual restraint, by blowing up anything and everything, and filling the few unoccupied patches of land in Gaza, with make-shift coffins.

Although we'd been shown satellite images of the port, and had been briefed on its layout, it still struck me as woefully inadequate for a city so heavily populated. We'd yomped across beaches and through shitty, holed streets all night, avoiding everyone, which took time. We dug in for a day's rest at the edge of the breakwater, as the sun snuck its tuft over the Mediterranean. It gradually revealed a harbour no bigger than some of the fishing ports I'd worked in my youth. Despite the increasing daylight, we could hear the Israeli attacks continuing inland, and it began to dawn on us that the op could be in trouble.

Day passed into night as we waited for the ship, one of us on sentry, three asleep. We had no firearms, but we were well-equipped for hand-to-hand combat. By the second night we were defecating in small bags, our bodies encrusted with salt, and we contemplated the looming need to eat discarded fish from the small boats, a few hundred yards away. We could not afford to get sick though, and of greater concern was our water supply. We knew that at some stage we'd have to break cover and fill our deflatable bottles.

Of course, the ship never did arrive. With Hamas pinging missiles, the Israelis had blockaded the shipping lanes, and were occupying sea space with their own war ships. Hungry for information, and sure now that extraction was the best course of action, we decided to make contact. Deniability was essential, so we had no military communication devices, just smartphones in watertight, commercially available cases. There were applications on them which encrypted or scrambled conversations, but Israel is on the ball with all comms, and we knew that any signal out of Gaza stood a more than an even chance of interception. Such concerns were secondary however, as we had to get a signal first, and it was clear that we wouldn't get one from our make-shift bunker on the breakwater.

I decided that I would go alone in search of what, at best, would be 2G. I cast off my kit, discarded all but the blade sheathed against my inner left leg, and headed for the city. My Arabic was pretty limited. I was confident with please, thank you, and excuse me, my three essentials for any deployment. I had hoped to secure comms long before I left the harbour, but like everything on that bloody Op, it went pear-shaped.

The glow from the smartphone screen lit my face every time I stroked it to life, and so I left a good five hundred metres between each check. That led me straight into Gaza City, and as I plunged deeper into its density, I became increasingly conscious that my bearings were becoming muddled. Anyone who grew up the way I did can sniff out the sea though, and I was confident that I would find my way back quickly. What I hadn't qualified for were the patrols.

The first one I encountered was a collection of three, each man carrying a heavy weapon. Rocket-propelled grenades were silhouetted over their shoulders like tulips before bloom. Hamas fighters, demonstrating to the population that they were prepared to take on the Apaches, Cobras, and whatever other helicopter gunships the Israeli Air Force had at its disposal.

This gaggle was far from alert. They smoked and talked, oblivious to my presence, as they passed less than two feet from me. Stupidly, I assumed that there would be spacing between the patrols marauding the streets. I emerged from a doorway and watched their backs weave around a corner, before igniting the screen on the smartphone. It turned out to be the best and worst action of that night. I immediately heard a shout as a second patrol picked up the glow and started barking orders at me. I assumed I was guilty of breaking some sort of curfew, and knew that it was fight or flight. There was no way I was going to talk my way out of it, and I certainly did not want to draw fire in such a crammed area. So I stood still, and decided to disable the men when they arrived.

The group arrived in one lump, as if they'd been glued together in a spittoon. That made my work so much easier. I placed the phone in the pouch above my coccyx, and eased one foot behind for stability. The patrol men noticed my stance and raised their arms immediately – an AK, and a homemade Carl Gustav pistol.

They came too close. They always do. Untrained assailants always believe a few metres to be sufficient distance to prevent an un-armed attack. Not only is that just wrong, it also narrows their options considerably. The Gustav weapon is dreadfully inaccurate, and a Klak is hard to handle. Of the three men, the only one with any wit appeared to have been issued a mortar tube.

What I didn't want was collateral damage – dead children in the houses on either side of me, or noise to attract anyone else to the scene. That meant the three men needed to be taken down hard, and that they would more than likely suffer permanent damage, or even die.

The youngest was the most excitable; perhaps he had most to prove. He gesticulated his Kalashnikov at me and, predictably, edged forward in the process. There was no shoulder butt on his model, so I dipped to the side and grabbed the barrel and mag to take his teeth out with the stock. I heard them shatter as I ducked and rose with my fist to hammer the holder of the Gustav with a disarming blow to the sweet meats. As he folded, the gun presented nicely and I twisted it from his grip, turning it on the leader, who was suddenly outnumbered by two guns to one. He gave up immediately, and crouched to his knees with his hands in the air. I walked behind him and kicked him in the back to make sure he was face down and unnerved at the prospect of what would happen next.

I set the guns down and incapacitated the younger man with a blow so heavy it could have killed him. The moaning of the second fighter had to be stopped, so I placed my knee across his shoulder blades and choked him until he too passed out. The leader panted and prayed, so I tore strips off his scarf and stuffed them into his mouth. I found cable ties on the belt of the second man, attached two together, and clicked them tight around his face, before securing his hands and feet similarly. Then I dragged each into a side street, and had to leave it at that. I needed to place distance between the scene and me, so I began a steady-paced run north. I knew the wounded men could be discovered within minutes, and that I needed comms immediately.

I had only covered about twenty metres when I saw yet another patrol, and realized that their station or briefing room must be close by. I was exposed; there was no obvious side street or gloom to shelter in, and my heaving chest betrayed my breath on the cold air.

The new patrol was different. I watched them as they rolled down the street, fingers parallel with their gun barrels, evidently much better versed and prepared than their predecessors. They were properly spaced, and I knew my luck had expired. I'd left one of their friends conscious, and I had visions of him flapping like a seal, head and tail raised as his pals went past. There was virtually no chance of evading capture, and less prospect of fighting my way out.

I had no need to run through my options. I'd done all of that before we got into the sea. Capture would be a nightmare. Hamas would assume I was Sayeret Matkal, the Israeli equivalent of our Special Reconnaissance Unit, or worse. Given the way I was dressed, they might assume me to be Shayetet 13, Israel's answer to my own SBS. Either way, I would be considered a prize hostage, or even an opportune candidate for slaughter and revenge, given the brutality of the air assault on Gaza. There was no way my own unit could claim me without upsetting Israel and the Palestinians, and the United States might not be too happy with the UK either. I was on my own.

The Hamas fighters spun on the balls of their feet, marking out sight lines and using what little light there was to clear the area. They were so much better than the previous unit. I began to wonder whether they had tried to make contact with the incapacitated men, and had taken the lack of response as an indicator of an incursion.

As the first man approached I pushed aside the urge to offer a gentle surrender. I was keen to avoid unnecessary shooting, but the risk that the hysteria of an arrest would lead to an instant execution was high. I'd seen tempers in the Arab world explode in a matter of seconds. I'd witnessed crowds goad gunmen into extra-judicial murder.

I stepped forward, but was immediately masked from the patrol when a door to my left was flung open. Instinct told me to pause, and I heard a woman barking at the men in what seemed to my un-trained ear to be faltering Arabic. I had no idea why the Hamas fighters were listening instead of firing, but their boots soon battered off a stream of echoes around the walls of the tight little street.

I had backed in behind the open door in the hope that the woman would simply close it again, and remain unaware of my presence. Instead, when the men were out of sight, I heard her speak. "I think you'd better come in."

Five

I'd never known the comfort of human contact in that way before. Death, when it often visited, had been on deployment. We almost expected to die. There were no hugs in the field. That is not to say that there was no reaction; there was always a reaction. Usually, more death. But to be smothered in hugs, as I was when I stepped off that flight, was a relatively new sensation, and was simultaneously comforting, and terrible.

First was Isla, who didn't run to me as I had expected. She walked slowly towards me, and raised her little arms for a lift. To bury my face in her neck and smell her hair was to finally acknowledge that her mother was dead. That was the point at which I nearly lost it. I felt her relief course through me like a shot of strong whiskey. I clung to her nearly as much as she did to me, a little limpet mine, threatening my detonation. I turned and twisted, unable to raise my face to Shannon's parents, who stood by patiently. Both were in tears, as were my own folks at their side.

Eventually, with Isla still on my shoulder, I walked towards my in-laws, and swung an arm around them too. I had never done more than shake her father's hand. A bear of a man, he hugged back and shook out his grief against me. Her mother, often given to emotion, was probably the steadiest of us all. Then came my parents, who uttered "so sorry son." My dad told me that there were reporters outside. At that point practicality returned, and I was able to compose myself. We needed a means to get out of the airport, and, well, that seemed like something I could usefully distract myself with.

I knew George Best Airport well. After we got married, Shannon and I decided to build a home in Northern Ireland, and ever since, I'd flown home a lot. Nesting perhaps. Preparing for Isla.

I knew there would be no easy exit past the press, so I told the others to leave and tell the reporters that I had missed the flight and would catch the next one. I watched through the sliding doors as the journalists gathered up their kits and wandered off. Then I strolled out over the flyover to re-join my family. I'd made a life's work of not having my photograph taken. I had exploited social media, but never been used by it. I was confident that I would not be recognised. In all honesty, I was relieved at the distraction, and the chance to get a breath. My heart hurt, and I promised myself that nothing would ever cause that to happen again.

For the next week, we were soaked in sympathy. Ordinarily, I would have shunned such intrusion. My intensely private nature could not have been more different from Shannon's. She made friends easily. Where I recoiled at a stranger's touch, she was huggy, touchy, happy. So it was that my parents' house became like an arrival terminal, as people I vaguely knew streamed through the door and crowded the rooms, grappling me and kissing Isla. The sheen on their faces reflected a loss which had evidently affected them deeply.

They were of a kind. Overseas aid or charity workers for the most part, those who picked up the pieces amid the destruction left by people like me. Contrary to my instincts, I found myself drawing huge comfort from their presence. They told me stories of my wife, of a life well-lived, of her importance on the planet. I took in with gratitude the tales of the little acts of kindness which she performed to make life valuable again, in places where the inflation of war had depleted its currency.

Isla never left my side, which was just as I wanted it. We slept at my folks' house, given the mess that forensics had left in our own. Eventually, I had to dose her with Calpol to make sure she'd sleep, while I performed an unavoidable task. I walked up to what had been our home, and stood in the living room to absorb what had happened there. It was one long, angry stand. Then I walked the half-mile to the house of horrors, the root of the evil that had taken my wife from our daughter. It had been emptied of the scum that had caused her to act as she had. The landlord, a local factory owner, had finally done what should have been done years earlier. I would have my time with that greedy bastard too.

I can't even bring myself to describe the funeral, other than to say that music can be a comfort, yes, but it can also draw the most insulated mind into the shuddering bleakness of bereavement. My wife had loved singing, and she eventually coated me with a blanket of country, turning steel guitar from a migraine-inducing screech, to a tolerable whine. It became an indication of her happiness. Any time I heard Waylon or Jonny blasting from the kitchen, I knew she'd be swaying around with Isla, laughing hard and smiling that beautiful smile.

Two days later I was back on a plane, my daughter at my side. She had no idea where we were going; I had no idea what she would think of my plan. But when we arrived at an obscure auctioneer's yard in Maidstone, Kent, she got it immediately. There, standing clear above the fence, was a 54-foot Norwegian-built cutter.

"Is that where we're going to live, Daddy?" she asked, her voice betraying excitement for the first time since I'd been home. In that moment, she sounded like a five-year-old again.

"It is, darlin," I replied, and climbed the fence as if it were a gnarly cargo net. I caught the panic on her face as I rolled over the barbed top edge. I spoke as I dropped to assure her that I was not about to leave her outside, then ripped the bottom edge of a weak spot, to let her through.

The hull would have been sound, had it not been for the pointless behaviour of the Customs officers, who had evidently just been given a budget for tungsten-tipped drill bits. Holes had been created every three feet, and the bulkheads had been torn out. She was still a beautiful craft though, spacious enough to live aboard, small enough to handle on my own. Isla's delight at finding a forward cabin sealed it.

"Daddy, it's so cool."

Because of the drug bust that had led to the boat's detention, there was TV interest at the auction, so I bid online. Fully aware that our house could take an age to sell, I was forced to use the money from my wife's life insurance, which didn't feel as bad as perhaps it should have. Over two weeks, with my dad and his charts and my father-in-law and his welder, we got her sea-worthy and sailed her home. Isla was with me every step of the way, making her new cabin cosy.

Gradually, Isla adapted. Every night we sailed to a different bay. My aim was to assure her that nobody would come for me, as they had for her mum. Nobody could find us, I told her, not if we kept moving.

She was given to panic in her dreams, and she often visited at night, tucking her toes against my back. I watched her those mornings as she woke, the horror dawning, then the ease creeping back in as she grappled for me. It gave me peace too. I needed her. I also needed to work out how I would support her financially, and how I could douse the hatred inside me for the man who had taken my wife.

Six

To this day I find it impossible to comprehend how we managed to meet that second time. She thought that perhaps God had sent me, but I was of the view that God would have sent her someone good, rather than someone useful. Particularly given the un-Godly use to which she would later put me. Perhaps she had a point; there are hundreds and hundreds of little streets in Gaza –nearly two million people live there, yet I managed to meet the same woman twice, in the space of a few days.

The door closed. She put her hand on my chest and walked me backwards through the tiny flat, her fingers to her lips in a command of silence. When she lifted the pressure, I stopped, and she reached behind me to open a rear door, and wound her upper body past me to look outside. I noticed her t-shirt sway, which betrayed the fact that she'd dressed quickly, and I caught the smell of sleep from her as she leaned across.

Satisfied that it was clear, she bid me outside where we dodged garbage and the stench of rotting meat, through what was little more than an open sewer. We walked for about three hundred metres before she turned and opened another door, and then waved me inside. I made my way as quietly as possible across the stone floor, and was grateful to hear her beautiful Irish accent again. "You're grand, there's nobody here."

"Who are you?" I asked.

"Who the fuck are you, more like?" she hissed.

I laughed out loud. She'd posed a fair question.

"I'm Shannon," she extended a hand. Her shake was strong.

Now, in normal circumstances, we don't tell anyone who we are or what we are doing, but these circumstances were not normal. She had saved my skin. I had saved a kid dying in her arms. She was obviously some sort of aid worker; I was obviously some sort of trouble. And finally, she was Irish, and I was Irish, and she was exceptionally beautiful. I resolved to lie through my teeth. The explosives we'd been sent to retrieve were at the front of my reasoning. Not only had the Semtex come from Ireland, it was concealed on an aid ship. I doubted it, but this woman could be the agent, the CHIS, the link between the IRA and Hamas.

We stared at one another. She held my gaze and bore through me. The dawn glow put warmth in her eyes. Never before, and never again will I experience anything like that connection. I could feel her heart, her compassion, her intensity, her kindness. I knew she was with me, and that she wouldn't ask again. "Well, whatever you're here for, you're in deep shit," she eventually broke the current.

I grunted agreement, and brought out my phone, hoping for a signal.

"Your make-up isn't very good. I knew you straight away, even just in the light of your phone" she said.

I let out a chuckle, grateful for her humour despite the dreadful mess that had been created. She was referring to my cam cream. Even then something told me that we wouldn't need to talk much. Something had been forged between this woman and I, on that beach, in the blood.

"Did the kid make it?"

"He did."

There were no thanks. There were none required. "I need to get a signal," I told her.

"No chance. Mobile network is the first thing that goes down when there's a fight. Israel controls the phone masts." I looked at her again, for quite a while. She looked right back, stripping me to the timber.

"I know where there's a sat phone, but I might need another favour," she said.

I could not have imagined what she would ask of me.

Seven

I find it easy to make decisions. Too easy, perhaps. I like to think that I follow my instincts, rather than my heart, because I worry that my heart can be as dark as my thoughts. Standing that night, looking at the yeti-like trail left in the fine, fingerprint powder that dusted our house, I tried to console myself with the notion that what I was about to do was no different than what Shannon had asked of me seven years before.

In the garage, I lifted the box of surgical gloves I kept for working with epoxy resin. I put one pair on, then removed another for later. I had a full-face dust mask hanging on the tool board, and a dozen cellophane dust suits, which Shannon had bought to protect my clothes against paint and filler. In the bathroom, I found the boxes of toiletries she and I had pinched from hotels around the word, and isolated the little shower caps.

Then I sat and planned my movements, just as I had done a hundred times before. For the first time in years, I would operate alone. To be without the responsibility of a Sergeant, or a Corporal, or a Marine, felt liberating. At 0330 I made my move, and walked the four miles to where the factory-owner lived. I knew he had migrant workers bunked up in his own house. That way he could charge them rent for the privilege, and the paltry pay he gave them would end up right back in his pocket.

I checked the ground for piercing objects, and in an obscured lane, placed the shower caps on my feet and head.

The dust suit made me look like a telly-tubby, but the mask must have made me look terrifying. Then I was free to put on the second pair of gloves, which I hoped would avoid any cross contamination; I was conscious that my DNA could have landed just about anywhere on the outward skin of the first pair.

It took me two minutes to get inside. I had no idea where the owner slept, so I eased around the spacious house gingerly. At 0400, I realized that my plan had a flaw. A mobile phone buzzed, then grew louder, until it became an alarm. There was movement, and a shuffle, then muffled conversation in Russian. Shift-work. The factory operation was enormous. The owner made his fortune from tourist trinkets which were sold in shops the length and breadth of the country. In green and gold and with folk ballads on a loop, these shops rammed fake Ireland down the throats of visitors. They in turn lapped up the little plaques and poems, and brought them home to their relatives as gifts. The irony was that they were made by Eastern Europeans in what was, in fact, part of the United Kingdom. And those poor bastards evidently worked around the clock.

Beside a bathroom was a door, which, I was grateful to discover, concealed an airing cupboard. Even through the mask I could smell the hygienic negligence of the bizarre accommodation arrangement. Inside, crushed against shelves, I bided my time and listened, as a small army readied itself for a day of painting stuff green. By 0430, all were gone.

I'll admit to being shocked when I opened the next door. The hump of a body in a bed led my eye toe-to-top where, eyes wide open, the factory owner lay, staring at me. Thankfully, he was alone. How he was not taken aback by my appearance, I don't know. I'd grown up in the area, he'd known me as a child, and he knew me now, despite the get-up.

"You're looking well, Sam," he said, without moving.

I almost laughed. The superior, sarcastic bastard. "Tell me where he is."

"Who knows," he said. "I employ them all through an agent."

"Then where's the agent?"

"He'll tell you nothing, Sam. He probably doesn't even know the man. The agent doesn't care for chick nor child. He beats them and batters them, and keeps them in line. I don't bother asking anything about them."

The carelessness in his tone scooped up my anger, as a child's hands might lift sand from a beach. He had known I would come, and I wondered if he knew what was about to happen to him. "Where's the agent?" I asked again.

He actually snorted. "Dublin, far as I know."

"You'll need to do better than that."

"Can't," was all he said, and I wondered whether he was resigned to his fate, or misunderstood his predicament. I'd always known how promiscuous he was, so I knew what was important to him. I stepped forward and with a following uppercut, caved his nose into his face. Then I tore back the festering duvet, and grabbed the triumvirate of his genitalia and gave it a full twist. To be fair, he gargled, but he didn't scream. If he hadn't grasped it before, he did now, as he laboured to gain composure, and shifted to persuasive mode.

"All right Sam," he panted, "all right, all right, I've got a number for him, I'll give you his number."

His face was awash with blood since his nose had ruptured. I didn't want him going anywhere for a phone or a pen, or a pad and paper. I gave his tackle another half turn, and with it came all that I needed. He gestured to a phone by the bed, and gasped the pin code. Then it was straightforward – contacts, name, address. I knew I wouldn't remember the phone number, and I resisted the urge to text it to myself, but the address was burned into my mind.

I debated leaving him there, in his stinking sheets, but I knew that at his age he wouldn't change. If I left him, he would get straight on the phone to the gang-master who had spirited away my wife's killer. I knew the police would have thirty suspects ahead of me. They all hot-bunked in his bloody house.

Contrary to what many believe of people like me, I *do* value life. In fact, I believe there to be nothing more important. But I understand that in order to allow decent people to lead a fair and worthwhile existence, those who would prevent that, need to be curtailed. I didn't kill him, but using a technique I had learned years before, I leaned forward and drew his tenure of abuse to a close.

*****

Destroying the coveralls and gloves was straightforward. This literally allowed me to blow smoke all over the place to prevent the plods from tracking me down. All day, every day, there was a fire burning at the edge of the sprawling factory.

There were acres of sheds, hundreds of workers, dozens of lorries. My face would have been one among many, in the dawn light. Upwind, I approached the bonfire, deposited my small bundle, and waited until it joined the factory waste as ash. The walk home gave me time to work out how to get to Dublin without being picked up on any cameras, or at the myriad of tollbooths.

Isla was still asleep when I got back. I washed well, and climbed in beside her, content that I had a plan to get to the gang master. I began to reason out my actions, imagining what Shannon would have made of it all. She had an uncanny knack of drawing out the dark stuff, and making me deal with it. She had never failed to find a way to persuade me that there was dignity or sense in my decisions. I craved that now. I ached for her guidance, as I closed my eyes.

And then I was staring at her, urging her to tell me what she wanted, and to give me the Sat phone. And I was willing her to feel the tremble inside that I was feeling, the type that can make a leg-stride falter. This was not just desire; it was dependence. Whatever had happened between us that night in Gaza, she made me feel like we already shared a past. My focus was shattered; I should have been concentrating on my team's extraction.

"Where are your men?" She'd obviously worked out the order of rank when we were on the beach.

"Not far. But I need comms. When can I get the phone?"

Her shoulders sagged. She turned her head to the wall, and gave up her own lie. "It's here. I'll get it."

Within five minutes I was on a flat roof. The kit was an old M4 Nera device. She explained that it was used by her aid agency to conduct radio interviews, to explain the impact of the conflict, and to raise funds. Making a voice call was exceptionally risky, but we had fail-safes. My conversation ought to sound civilian, to any eavesdropper. I called the number, spoke to a desk clerk, used my cover ID, and disconnected. Five minutes later I dialled again. The clerk had done his job and got someone senior enough to take directions, and relay a message.

This man talked to me as a brother might, delighted to hear from me. He then read what he claimed to be a phone number for "where mum was staying." I tapped the numbers into my phone. I knew that among the digits were co-ordinates. We made small talk, and ended the call. Then I entered a scramble of random numbers on the keypad, just in case the woman behind me wasn't what I thought she was, in order to prevent a re-dial.

"Ok," I told her. "In an hour, I'll come back, and we'll sort out whatever it is you need in return."

Incredibly, she accepted that at face value, and I left her there on the roof.

The co-ordinates took me a mile inland, to a confusingly non-descript street. I wondered for a while what the significance of the location was, but it was only upon consulting the numbers saved to my phone that the penny dropped. An image of a partial cake slice had appeared on the screen. I had a wireless connection.

It took me ten minutes to stabilize the app, to type the message, encrypt it, and get it away. It took another fifteen minutes to receive a response. It was far from expected. Rather than an extraction plan, we were told that the aid ship had been re-routed to Ashdod, an Israeli port outside the Gaza cage. I was being ordered to get there, finish the job, and then extract from the Israeli coast.

On first read, it felt like lunacy. I pulled up a map on the smartphone, battered in the Lat and Long on the GPS, and my heart sank. We had no boats, and no chance of breaking through the IDF's land border security. Ashdod was not a swim away either. It was at least 25 miles by sea. I entrusted the next move to my instincts. I knew a plan would form. My unit was safe and dry in the harbour, and the draw of that woman sucked me back through the streets, to fulfil a promise.

I woke from the intense doze with a start. I'd been out for just ten minutes. I hate superstition, I have no time for planet alignment or karma or any other such stuff, but I am not immune to it. I looked at my daughter, sleeping soundly for a change, and took the dream as confirmation. The factory worker exploited people. I told myself that there would soon be fewer people who could take advantage of kids just like Isla. And then I slept.

Eight

Every snippet of information leads somewhere, if it is properly interrogated. I told myself that what I was about to do was for my daughter, and for my wife. In some respects, it was. I needed to know that what had been done to them could not be done to anyone else. But I also needed to strangle the hurt inside me, and revenge seemed like a good first step. The way things worked out, that proved correct. All manner of problems were solved by my actions that week, and all manner of problems were created.

Boat ownership in Ireland is generally a pretty thankless pursuit. The weather is good for about two months of the year, and not always the same two. There are sheds up and down the country where boats hibernate for up to nine months. I knew this from years spent sanding, painting, rigging, and delivering boats all around the Irish coast. I also knew of a nearby yard, where two dozen suitably fast examples would be standing.

I was determined that nothing would place me in Dublin. A significant part of the SBS post-selection training had focused on surveillance. Some of what we'd been taught brought deviousness to a whole new level. The courses had reinforced just how difficult it was to avoid detection, and at that point, I was grateful for them.

I borrowed my dad's car, as it was petrol, and filled it to the throat at the local store. CCTV footage of me filling a car could not arise suspicion; similar images of me stockpiling fuel in barrels would certainly become evidence in any future court case. Then I gathered together every jerry can and container I could find, and drove the lot into our garage. Well, my garage. I syphoned almost every drop out of the car and into the containers. That night I deposited them at the high-tide mark in a quiet cove, a few miles away.

*****

I tucked Isla in, under the care of her grandparents, and went back to the garage. There I kitted up, grabbed my old bike, and cycled the three miles to the boatyard. It didn't take long to get into the shed, and to identify a fifteen-foot rigid inflatable, with a nice Yamaha 115 horsepower outboard engine on the back. I rolled the RiB down the slipway and hauled the trailer back to the shed, leaving the boats as I had found them, minus one. Gloved, balaclava'd and in a full dry-suit, I tossed the bike aboard, skulled off shore, dropped the outboard and made gentle progress to pick up the fuel.

Fully stocked, I broke for open water, and was soon planing at 30 knots down the East Coast, towards Dublin Bay. Customs posed a concern, but even if I was pulled up and boarded, I had nothing on the boat that would warrant investigation. All I really required for this job was determination, possibly Google maps, and my bare hands.

Years before I'd done maintenance jobs in the pretty little Bullock Harbour, near Dalkey, on Dublin's gold coast. I reckoned that was anonymous enough for my needs. I went over and over the timing in my head. It was dark now, and it would have to be dark when I arrived. By the chart, I reckoned it was 135 miles. At 30 knots that would take me just under four hours, and with daylight Greenwich Mean Time, I anticipated landing at the perfectly dormant 0400.

There was a stiff South Easterly blowing when I crossed Dublin Bay, which allowed me to tie the RiB outside the harbour wall, largely out of sight, and in slightly deeper water. I hoped that might allow me to leave in a hurry, or at a time of my choosing. If I got it wrong, the boat would be beached and I'd be at the mercy of the flood tide.

Under the dry suit, I wore paint-spattered jeans and a scabby old fleece. I rolled up a face buff and a scruffy cap, intending to pass as a construction worker. I slung the bike over my shoulder, and scaled the slippery surface of the wrong side of the harbour wall. It took me an hour of enjoyable cycling to get to the north inner city, my view of Dublin Port and the East Link undisturbed. I crossed the Liffey and made my way a few streets in towards Mountjoy. At that point, I had to consult my phone for directions.

The address the factory owner had given me was an apartment near Summerhill, and when I looked at the street layout, I was glad I'd opted for the pushbike. It was anonymous, and it allowed me to get in and out of the area without having to cross a carriageway, or get snarled in the one-way traffic system.

The apartment complex was almost u-shaped in appearance. Time was tight, so I didn't spend the amount of time I should have conducting a proper recce. I cycled in past an ornamental roundabout and quickly identified the correct staircase. What I should have done was stop some distance away, and work my way in gradually, listening and watching. Had I done that, things would undoubtedly have turned out very differently.

I climbed the stairs as if they were my own, to remove any possibility of being mistaken for a thief. That's why I had my head down, and the cycle and the stairs meant that my heart was pumping in my ears. It wasn't until I got to the top of the two flights that I caught a muffled commotion. My eye was drawn along a landing and as sure as eggs are eggs, it was coming from the bloody apartment I intended to visit. So much for surprising the gang-master in his sleep.

I walked towards the door, and as I passed I heard a scream and a slap, followed by dull thuds and sobbing. Convinced a woman was being attacked, I put my shoulder to the door, and bounced back off it immediately. Now, I'm no bodybuilder, but I was just out of theatre, and as fit as a trout. I'm six feet tall, fifteen stones, and although some would say rugged, I know I'm brutal in appearance. But I carry no excess, and I have never put my weight to a domestic doorframe and seen it stand up, so I knew that this house had been prepared for unwelcome visitors.

I needn't have worried. My attempted intrusion was immediately answered. The door opened before me, and there, in glorious underpants and a wife-beater vest, stood a suave-looking mountain of a man. For the second time in the space of a minute, I questioned my luck. I registered his features as quickly as possible, knowing that a battle was inevitable. His shoulders bulged from recent exertion, as he leaned forward into the doorframe, one hand on each edge. The fingers on one were ornamented with gold, and slathered in blood. This was eighteen stones of pure ignorance. He was plainly unperturbed, confident, and mistaken. Go now, or wait for him to move? I decided to try to draw him out of his comfort zone.

"I've called the Guards," I said, imagining that he would assume I was a neighbour.

"Good, good," he replied, which was not really what I had hoped for, to be honest. "Then they can take yer one away for harassment."

I noted how well he had assimilated Dublin parlance, his Eastern European tone was mixed with more than just a little of the vernacular. He ducked and turned his head to peer under his colossal arm, and I followed his gaze to find a woman in black crawling towards a sofa, gripping its arm. He curled in further to shout at her, and as he did, his right hand dropped off the steel doorframe.

He began to tell her not to bleed on his furniture, so I stepped left and used my entire body weight and both arms to take his hand and give his wrist a full turn anti-clockwise, breaking it immediately and dislocating his elbow in the process. It's a simple enough move, but one rarely gets the opportunity to perform it, as human strength is all focused on beating counter-intuitive movements. It is also excruciatingly painful. Some wounds are so severe that they cut through the messages being sent to the brain, and this often leaves a combatant able to go on. The trick is to do just enough damage to ensure that the pain endures. I needed him to remain conscious, but disabled, and I needed to be able to inflict more pain to get the answers I had come for.

A heavy blow to the side of his throat forced him back inside the apartment, and I got a chance to close the door. I stared at the woman, who was gradually recovering. It's always a worry to intervene in a domestic. I understand why it happens, but it's curious that in such situations a person being saved from a savage beating can turn violently against a Samaritan. I kept an eye on the woman to see what way she might go, as the thug laboured for breath at my feet. There was a certain comfort, however, in her next comment.

"Thank you," was all she managed, but it was clear that she was Irish, and something about her made me think that she was not a sex worker, or a domestic slave. Perhaps it was because she was well enough dressed, understated, practical. Someone under duress would be forced to dress provocatively, or have no choice but to wear clothing provided to them, from a discount store like Lidl or Aldi.

Her facial wounds were limited to a cut across the temple, which was bleeding hard, and a rapidly blossoming black eye. I could tell by the way she attempted to cradle herself that the bastard on the floor had gone to work on her torso. Perhaps he was a boxer or a martial artist. They tend to wear down the trunk, varying and concealing their punishment.

I was confident that the thug was sufficiently incapacitated, so I stepped on his face as I walked over him to help her up. She was sore, but I needed to know more about what was going on. "Anyone else in this flat?"

"I don't think so," she said. "I only got here a bit before you did."

"Any weapons?"

"I'd be amazed if there weren't," she wheezed.

"Does he live alone?"

"I don't know," she said.

"So, who are you?" I asked, becoming slightly annoyed that she appeared to know so little.

"I'll tell you in a minute. Can you get me out of here?" It was her turn to be exasperated. She made a fair point.

"Yes, sorry, I will, but you'll need to give me some time with him."

I cleared the rest of the flat, all three rooms of it, and returned to the woman. "This isn't gonna be pretty. Can you wait in the jacks?" I held the door to the bathroom open.

"I will in me bollocks," she said, and nodded to the bloke on the floor. "Do whatever you have to do."

This was not ideal. I didn't want anyone else to hear what it was that I needed to know. That would lead to identification, which would lead to the factory owner, which would lead to Portlaoise Prison, which would leave Isla alone again. "Get in the fucking bogs, or I leave you here with him."

My tone was deliberately harsh, but she was fit for it, and shrugged, painfully. I got the impression that there was a long history between the pair, and that she wanted to watch.

Dear knows how much she heard as I went to work on him. It seemed to take forever, and I was deeply worried that the noise would rouse a neighbour and bring the police. He was both physically and mentally tough, but he had no ideological commitment to a cause. Taliban fighters might be inept and weak, but their minds are strong. Their information is tough to tap, because they believe that what they're doing is right. This big bastard had no such emotional attachment to his work, and once he realised that my demands were deeply personal, he understood that I wouldn't be leaving him alive unless he choked out the details. We got there in the end.

Then I had a decision to make. Disable, or decommission. I couldn't pull my little factory-owner stunt on him; that would link the two incidents. I couldn't kill him either, unless I killed the witness too, and I had no intention of murdering the woman. So I went for two simple enough fixes. The first was disgusting, but took the sex out of him forever. The second ensured that he would never raise his fists in anger again. I then took the woman from the bathroom, and tried to debrief her. That proved tricky, as she juked around my head to try to get a view of the now-sobbing mound on the floor.

"We're leaving now, and we need to do so quietly."

"What did you do to him?"

"He's alive," I said, and watched her shoulders sag a little. "We need to go. How did you get here?"

"I drove."

"Can you drive now?"

"What do you think?" she said.

I didn't think that was a good idea. She could barely raise her arms. "If I leave you outside, will you call the cops?"

"For what reason would I call the Guards? What would I say to them? That I came to get a girl from a pimp and he beat the shit out of me, and then some fella from the North came and cut his bollocks off?" She was incredulous.

"I didn't cut his bollocks off," I said, but turning to match her gaze, I did notice how his shorts were absorbing blood, as a tea towel might a drink spill. It was definitely time to go. "Look, I'll drive you to a hospital, I hope you've a car with a big boot."

It was a hairdresser's car. I lowered her into the passenger seat, and got my bike. I released the front wheel, and had to leave the back one sticking out the rear. "Where's the hospital?"

She began to give me directions, but when we passed the Mater Emergency Department, I began to wonder where she was taking us. Ordinarily I would have invested some server time in keeping track of our direction, speed and where the sun would rise. But the woman was blethering away and because Google makes us lazy, I knew I could rely on a backup. What I didn't have was much darkness left, so I was keen to get this sorted, and to start moving towards the boat.

"I could use someone like you," she began. "You obviously know what that bastard was up to."

"All I know is he brings in foreign workers, and skims them."

"Illegals too, mostly women," she said. "He brings them over, promises cleaning or office work, and within an hour of being picked up at Dublin airport, they've been raped at least twice."

I stayed silent, but felt fairly satisfied that he'd been neutered.

"They're in houses just like these," she winced as she raised her arm to gesture at the Georgian terraces sweeping past. "And the gregarious men of Ireland enjoy them every day, whether they're drugged of half dead. They don't give a rat's ass."

None of this surprised me. I'd seen it all before, in Helmand, in Poole, in Palestine. Flashes of my wife appeared before me. I swiped them away as if an advert had popped up on my phone, but the image kept bouncing back. I knew then that I wouldn't make the tide.

We coasted into the North inner city, along yet another beautiful street. I detest towns. I cannot abide the claustrophobia and proximity to people that city life insists upon, but Dublin is different. There is space in Dublin. The streets are broad, the houses simple but statuesque, and the architecture is untouched by bombing missions or terrorism. I have always felt at ease in the Pale. It always felt to me that there was mischief around every corner.

This woman, though, was rapidly destroying that image for me. She was talking about the "shitheads" who spent their wages on exploited women. She insisted the Johns must know that the victims had been trafficked. She talked about drugs, and crime gangs, and how useless the Gardaí was. Then suddenly she yelled at me to turn right, as if I had made a stupid mistake. There followed a hard left and a long lane, a set of plush gates and eventually an austere old convent.

This was a scary-looking place, and I immediately pitied the children who had been educated – or incarcerated – in such an imposing place. We walked up a stone staircase, and it was plain to me that this woman had no intention of going to hospital. She was reinforcing every point, like she was pitching to me. Along a corridor we reached a small, barren office. She flicked on a fan heater and muttered that the nuns would not be happy if they knew she had it. Organised religion and misery in Ireland once went hand in glove.

Over three hours we talked, or rather I listened, and I dressed her wounds. In the Marines, a body is a body, a machine of sorts, and where there is damage we get in there and try to fix it. I had forgotten the niceties of civilian life, and when I checked her over, she seemed to panic slightly as I examined her ribcage and her spine. I stopped when

I realised, a little too late, that she was alarmed. After a moment, she relented, but I was suddenly conscious that her crusade against abuse might have been borne of personal experience. I decided that if anything was broken, it couldn't be too serious, given the rate she was rattling on. I became less aware of what she was saying, as of the spark in her eyes, and through it I followed the shake and nod of every heartfelt gesticulation. Her commitment inevitably made me think of my dead wife, and I knew that whatever this woman was working up to, I would help her achieve.

And that's where Charlie started; my secret company, my means of income, my pathway from perdition. But I had to get to Lithuania first, and make another withdrawal before I could start depositing in any absolution account.

Nine

Shannon is the only person to have seen inside my mind, and understood. Shannon *was* the only person, I mean. That became fully apparent following a shameful incident in Belfast, while I was home on leave. She consoled me afterwards, and looking back now, I do wonder if she thought it was, perhaps in part, her fault.

Against all odds, my R&R had fallen over Christmas. It was the first time I'd had the chance to spend it with Isla since she was born, and only the second Christmas I had spent with Shannon. I received a tap on my shoulder one morning as we prepared to patrol from a forward operating post. It was the dustiest, dirtiest, most dangerous compound we'd occupied all tour. I was filling in my hole, the one I'd slept in for two weeks, dug by my own giant paw. The sand bag walls of our makeshift fort were all we had to protect us; well, that and some pretty heavy general-purpose machine guns, a truckload of artillery and a mortar team.

Anyway, I was told that a keen Lieutenant had arrived, was being flown to the outpost, and could take over from me. With hindsight, I wondered whether someone, somewhere had realized how much time I'd spent on the ground, and how many of my men had been sent home without legs. We'd had a hell of a tour, and although we had taken out a dozen Taliban positions, their land mines had literally crippled us.

My troop was blisteringly brutal, probably among the best few sections of Royal Marines I'd ever served with. The young ones were brave and smart, the Corporals and Sergeants across the board were experienced and committed. During larger Ops, we'd managed to trim the Taliban right back without losing a single Bootneck. But it was the bloody IEDs that took the toll. I had applied tourniquet after tourniquet, on one occasion three to the same man. It was horrific. I lost count of the number of times I'd knelt by one of my men as they growled to suppress the shock of seeing their limbs in sinew beside them. When it happened, I couldn't stop my mind springing to that song by Shane MacGowan. I used to love that song, "A Pair of Brown Eyes," but I don't know why it came to me as the arms and legs of other men lay scattered all around. I looked to the sky and wondered how the hell the juke-box of my drinking days had become the theme track to my career.

There were occasions when it was simply too dangerous to let the medics close to the maimed. One man down is bad, two explosions ought to be preventable. It went against general orders, but in my mind, it was sensible; better to lose the boss than the medic. So, insisting that the doc retrace his steps with the rest of the section, I tended the armless, the legless, the blind and insane, as Shane would say. My reasoning was that they could make it back without me, but that without the expertise of the morphine man, they might not make it back at all. It was a way of alleviating the guilt associated with leading men to their deaths. The responsibility was mine. I was in my 30s, and in Bootneck terms, I'd been around the block. No matter how brave they were, the men in my unit were scared at times. People often confuse the two. Bravery is not fearlessness. Bravery is the suppression of fear to accomplish what you think needs to be done. My men had loads of it, but they trusted me to make the right decisions. No detector can trace every mine though; no section can sweep ahead of every footstep. Those crippled were on my conscience, while my hands and feet, remarkably, remained with me.

As forty loomed closer than thirty, I began to feel my back stiffen. The Bergen never got any lighter, and my kit seemed to be permanently saturated in the blood of others. Countless times I'd hauled the heads and torsos of brave little Marines to heli-vacs, in the full knowledge that if the catastrophic bleed didn't take them, the PTSD might. I knew too that I would get it, but I didn't have time to contract anything back then. Contrary to what the press might say, Post Traumatic Stress is treated pretty seriously in the Corps. I always looked upon it as a kind of virus, or a cold, that would inevitably spread throughout my troop. My view was that I couldn't catch it until that dreadful tour was finished, but I never doubted that it would come.

It wasn't until that Christmas that the cracks began to appear, and let the darkness in. It started with fear, which was hard to take, frankly. It came at night, was triggered in sleep, and was dreadful. Some talk of flashbacks, others of re-living the hell. For me, closing my eyes was like going to the movies. Everything was so vivid, so real, and yet so embarrassingly ordinary, once the sun rose. Darkness, for a period, became my enemy, and I can't fully explain why. Perhaps it was because, for the most part, death had visited at night; when an allied army unit got their range wrong, and blew the shit out of our position, then denied it. Or when we were too fresh to the field to understand how the Taliban was working in any given area.

Anyway, panic was unusual to me. I'd wake hard, eyes wide open, ready to burst out, and realise that sleep had taken me to hell again. But the anxiety didn't end there. It endured for hours, as I lay awake and listened and jerked; I was frightened, and I am virtually never frightened. Even under extreme fire, even with bits of Bootneck hanging from rocks or plastered over walls, I was not frightened. But there is no adrenaline to protect you at night, in bed, beside your wife. There is no rifle or General Purpose Machine Gun with which to appease your fear and shoot up the enemy. There is just silence, and darkness, and cowardice. And it crept through me like the dawn over sea, enveloping and exposing me, and, according to my wife, making me human again.

Isla and I were happy, hand in hand, on an elevator in Belfast's Victoria Square shopping centre. The plan was to buy her mother a Christmas present, and Isla was full of chat. I always scan, I can't help it. I'm not saying I'm ultra-alert or anything, but I take in my surroundings, probably seeking out threat, and making sure I have the capacity to react. Ahead of me was a man who was turned astern, looking past me, at my little girl. His mouth was open like a hyena, his tongue wide and flat, his head nodding slightly. There was no doubt in my mind, he was a slobbering, salivating pervert who had forgotten himself, and was ogling my child. This guy's leery desire immediately took me back to the Middle East, and a cacophony of rage rose in me, like he'd tossed a grenade into a bunker.

The moving stairs reached his feet as I reached for him, plucking him from the ground and throttling him back against a glass wall.

"Fuck are you looking at?" was all I could manage to growl, my teeth ground shut in anger, his body giving way to shock and fear. Then there was screaming and slapping and Isla was crying and the man was in a mess on the ground. Somebody called for security and two women arrived and were right in my face calling me for every name they could muster. I lifted Isla up and drew her in and turned to walk away, and it was only then that I realised what I had done.

"He's got a learning disability you bloody animal!" I heard a woman shout.

Somehow, I knew it was the man's sister. I turned back again and looked at the scene, people gathered around him. All I could see were his feet. The other woman could have been his mum. She was distraught and wailing beside him. My eyes closed as my heart sank, and a swollen ball of nausea travelled up my chest. I had the overwhelming urge to return and plead an apology, but I could see the sister would wear none of it.

"What's *wrong* with you?" she screamed, incredulous.

And then I prioritised. I chose Isla over my conscience, and I turned and left, holding her tight and saying over and over again that everything would be all right, ignoring her questions about why I had hit that man. I don't even remember hitting him, I don't know if I did. If she was right, I knew he could be in real difficulty. I took her away.

There were still tears and terror and snot when we got home. Isla ran straight to her mother and told her everything in one great diatribe of distress. Shannon looked at me in horror, and then relented, as it dawned on her that remorse, rather than anger, was my main affliction. She calmed Isla down, as only she could back then, and later she coaxed it all out of me. I made no reference to the excuse that tried to force itself out, to mitigate my behaviour, but she somehow sensed that there was precedent for what I had done, and that she had been complicit in it.

She reasoned it out, truthfully. Had she tried to shower me with shit and niceties, I would have had no comfort. But she drew me to a conclusion of sorts, without letting me off the hook.

"You fucked up today," she began, which was cutting, but necessary.

"I know, I'm sorry Shan. It's just there, it's in me."

"That's why it won't be the last time. You'll do it again, but you need to address it each time, to feel the hurt. Then maybe it will happen less often."

"Don't hold back, Shan, will you love?"

"No point, Sam. You need to realise that other people aren't like you. You've been surrounded by commandos for years, hon, so it's not your fault that you're tuned to the fucking moon. But if you're going to get out, you're going to have to learn to live like us. Not everyone is the enemy. There isn't risk 'round every corner. And you need to realise that other people are no match for you. They chucked in red meat and wanted you to come out cross. Now you have to re-train for ordinary life."

I stared at her. I knew she was right, but I didn't know how to get there.

"What you did was out of love and protection."

I snorted.

'It was, Sam. Your instincts are good, to protect Isla, to look after me. But your instincts are to fight *immediately*. You need to fight clever, you need to consider that fighting isn't the first and only option. You have to get used to being around different types of people, gentle people, confused people, folk who aren't familiar with fast decisions and quick reactions. That man must have been so scared when he saw you coming at him today."

"He was terrified, God love him," I rasped, as the shame overwhelmed me. And then it came. I told her of the sleepless nights, of the horrors in the dark, of the weakness I felt. Shannon drew out the pain like a syphon, and when the flow began it was hard to stop. In the end, I even told her of the dreams in which I had imagined harming her and Isla. She assured me that I didn't scare her, that she felt safe with me, and that she was sure I would never hurt them. The relief, eventually, was enormous.

That was the beginning of my final extraction from the Marines, of a phased dislocation, designed to make me a normal man again. And then the person who shackled me to sanity was murdered, and I needed to find a way to do it, alone.

Ten

"Swimmer canoeists" was how members of our service were once known. Back then it was called the Special Boat Squadron, and during the war the stuff those guys got up to was genuinely heroic. Having been dropped into the sea from a submarine, with virtually no kit, and balls as big as mangos, they raided and bombed all over Europe. Their canoes were flimsy and slow, and they even greased their heavy woollen jumpers to try to keep themselves warm when they swam. It seemed like madness to us when, during our own training, we were regaled with stories of their exploits. At least, it seemed that way then; it didn't so much now.

I stared at the boats that Shannon had obtained for us. The team I was leading was made up of four highly-trained kayakers, who could blast rapids and paddle for two days without sleep. But that was in Navy-issue boats. What I was looking at were dangerous canvas-coated tubs, with no spray deck to keep the water out, and little legroom. Each man in my team was a big unit. in fact, at fifteen stones I was the smallest. How we were going to navigate around the might of the Israeli navy in these yokes was beyond me. I dated the tubs to the seventies, and despite my reservations, I thought back to what our predecessors had achieved, and rather imagined that they would have envied our craft.

The whole thing seemed full of irony, and I couldn't help but smile to myself as I mused over what I was about to ask my men to do. Our call sign was Charlie. Yet because we had been deployed covertly behind the lines of an ally, we were deniable, and therefore had no radio. I thought of a line from the movie, Apocalypse Now, "Charlie don't surf." I looked up from the kayaks to the rolling waves crashing up the beach, and begged to differ. In these daft little boats, Charlie was indeed about to surf, all the way to the most militarised waters in the Mediterranean.

I still look back on that Op with mixed feelings. It was on that deployment that I found my wife. It was on that deployment that Shannon and I removed a threat to decency. But it was on that Op that I got busted back to a Bootneck. Don't get me wrong – the effort, work and pride that had gone into earning a Green Beret was enormous. The endurance and pain we had gone through will never leave me. But a few years later I'd done it all again, only in a more extreme form, to progress through Special Forces selection and get my SBS badge. My wife and I later came to refer to that operation as '"the Ashdod incident."' After it, the sense of achievement associated with having made it into the Special Boat Service, was stripped from me; with the taking of one conscious decision, and one life.

The sea state was shocking, beyond "marginal." Had we been training, I'd have pulled the plug. Plenty of our number had died above or below the sea, and it seemed to me that we stood a pretty fair chance of adding to that toll. My only consolation was that if we were careful, there was virtually no way our matchbox-like vessels would appear on any Israeli radar.

There was a certain satisfaction when the burn began in my shoulders, as the muscle memory kicked in and I shovelled the running sea beneath me to climb over the breakers. After ten minutes, we had each got beyond the rip, and we paused to muster and sponge out. The kayaks were tippy, and rolled all over the place. Their round hulls made them hard to steer, but we got in phase with their peculiarities after a while, and the six-hour paddle gave me time to process what the woman had done for us, and asked of me.

I had hoped that her eagerness to help me was inspired by the connection I felt to her. Those eyes had captivated me, and that woman stayed in my sights as I reached and hauled the paddle. She dulled the pain in my trapezius, deltoids and triceps.

I had insisted on a tandem configuration. Four kayaks in a straight line was the safest way to avoid losing one another, but it was also the surest way to be detected. To an observer, from the air or satellite, a line could be mistaken for a larger vessel. So we opted for pairs, and I trusted the other team to look out for one another, just as my buddy and I were doing. It seemed inevitable that there would be capsizes, but Eskimo rolls in these ramshackle boats would only result in a sinking. We would need one another to invert and empty the canoes of water, before clambering back in.

My main concern though, was to work out how I might complete the task that Shannon had set me. I'd briefed the others on what we would do when we arrived at the port, but I hadn't told them that I would be vanishing again.

Shannon was tough, headstrong, and committed, a bad combination. I insisted that she involve nobody else, but she ignored me. I tried to negotiate, but I had nothing to offer. I stood in her flat, on the marble floor with its fine dusting of sand, and eventually accepted everything she requested. It seems like madness now, but she was so compelling and so determined that hers was the right course of action. All I was asking for were some small boats – what she was demanding was totally out of whack.

"He's a predatory paedophile," she said, failing to understand my reluctance. "He rapes kids, surely you can see the sense?"

I stared at her, frustrated at being side-tracked like this. "I have to get my team into Israel, and out of the Middle East as quickly as possible. This is not what I'm here for," I explained, but I knew this was a mistake as soon as I said it.

"Well, what *are* you here for?" she countered. I closed my eyes, paused, and dismissed the question.

"I need the boats."

"And I need a favour, and you appear to be the type of person that can help me with this, and frankly, if you don't, then you and your little band of brothers are on your own-ee-oh."

I will always remember that phrase. It was said to me when I was wee, and it wedged a little space in my mind. "Well, where is he?" I must have resigned myself to her request about this man.

"He's in Jerusalem, probably."

"Jerusalem's a long bloody way from Ashdod."

"It's two moons by camel," she said, which again nearly made me laugh, given the country we were in. "But for someone who is proposing to ignore a naval blockade, international protocol, and the might of the Israeli Defence Forces, I should think that would be a piece," she paused, "of piss."

This woman seemed to have a dictionary at her disposal. Her access to vocabulary unbalanced me ever after. Words just appeared to devote themselves to her. She seemed to have a capacity to pluck the pertinent phrase from the air in front of her, and insert it into any argument, as if stacking pigeonholes in a post room. She could gut any adversary. I gave up.

"So, I find him, in the middle of a major city, and..."

"You'll find him no problem because he's at the U.N. building." She had an answer to everything.

"And then what?"

"And then you do what you do," she said, rather matter of factly.

"I kill him?"

She just stared at me. I stared back. It seemed pretty clear that she wanted me to kill him.

"So, a senior figure in the U.N. peacekeeping outfit turns up dead, and the Israelis ignore it?"

"Not the point," she said. "Point is, he won't be able to abuse children every time he comes to Gaza under the pretence that he is here to help them."

"And you have evidence that this guy is doing this?"

"Well, if you want to hang around, I can bring you half a dozen little boys who have been left bleeding by this bastard. If you want to hang around, I'll bring you their distraught parents. If you want to listen to how their lives have been ruptured like their...." She paused, and choked up, and I relented.

"Ok," I said. "But why doesn't someone here just take him out? Hamas or someone?"

"Cause he's dishing out money, and he's feeding families, and he's supplying hospitals and he's the dog's balls to the right people. You think this place is any less vulnerable to corruption than any other hell hole on earth?"

I said nothing. It was a well-trodden path, that of the paedophile. I was broadly aware of all that had occurred in my own country, how those attracted to children had insinuated themselves into positions of moral superiority, in order to feed their addiction. I had never managed to understand how anyone could justify satiating their own desires, when the distress of children was evident. They often claimed to believe that what they were doing was not wrong, but the lengths to which they went to cover it up always suggested otherwise.

"So, do you want the boats?" she pressed.

"Yes."

"A friend will bring them to the harbour tonight."

"I asked you not to involve anybody else," I said.

"Well, I'm not carrying the bloody boats, and you lot can't very well walk around Gaza in your cargo pants and face paint, can you?" This woman was infuriating, and stunning.

"You trust this bloke?"

"I don't trust anyone really. But yes, he's not about to bust your bollocks."

I did wonder whether her Irishness was part of the attraction. Almost everything she said reminded me of home. It felt as if there was a point of reference for us, right from the outset. She made me smile, like we had a secret language.

And so it was set.

I was soaked. And chafed and rashed. Every bloody job I did as an officer in the SBS seemed to result in the extremities being punished. Feet, fingers, arse, sack. The unhappy quartet that often froze, rubbed or blistered under extreme conditions. The sponging of water kept the crotch sodden with salt water, like we were ladling pain onto our penises. The rubbing of the caked salt had built up abrasion as I pulled stroke after stroke, distracted as I was by running through the various scenarios with Shannon. What if she was trying to stroke me? Could this be a woman scorned who wanted an ex-lover removed? I honestly didn't think so, but I had no evidence of the man's offenses. I had no idea how I would even manage to get to Jerusalem; I had never been there before. I had never been to Israel, or Palestine for that matter.

I have always taken a read on the people I meet, and tried to remain realistic about them. Nobody is without flaws, least of all me. I erred towards trust, which was a weakness, and I was aware that the woman had caught my breath, and sucker-punched me, and that made me vulnerable. After all, *she* could be the contact who was due to receive the old IRA explosives, *she* could be a militant sympathizer. She could be a bloody Hamas operative for all I knew. I traced her, her ability to speak Arabic, a white Irishwoman in a war-torn state, giving aid, in possession of a satellite phone. Had I not already fallen in love with her, I would very likely have placed her at a remove from us in one way or another. Little wonder my team was incredulous at my decision to accept her help, and to carry on with that ridiculous operation.

But thoughts of her made the paddle pass more easily. Like the horrendous yomping of my training days in Devon, I allowed my mind to carry me away as my body thundered pain signals towards my brain. My legs could be screaming at the inferno burning in my thighs, but my mind could counter it. It was on the crest of such distractions that we arrived at Ashdod, an industrial, stinking port on Israel's South West Coast. The sea was alive with plastic and detritus, and we picked up bag after bag on our paddles as we lapped quietly around an enormous breakwater. We entered a vacuous harbour with multiple berths, and an astonishing military presence. It was going to be a challenge to even locate the correct ship without being caught, never mind getting aboard and removing the explosives.

During other operations, I would have had a wetsuit-waistcoat full of flares, and a kit. Inside the kayak would be my rifle of choice, an L119 carbine, the stubby little C8. I'd also have a handgun, a Sig usually. We couldn't deploy with any of that though. All we had were our dry suits, boots, and fins. We stood next to no chance.

Eleven

I was at an enormous disadvantage. I could not speak Lithuanian. Nor had I any Russian, other than the capacity to order two beers and to inquire of strangers whether *they* spoke English. At least Lithuanians used the Latin alphabet. When I marauded the Russian caucuses, it was particularly hard to find my way around, because of the Cyrillic script on the road signs. A young woman came to my aid on the plane to Vilnius, though. She was a bubbly, friendly girl with a pretty, portly face, who tried to strike up a conversation from the moment of buckle-up.

"Hello, how are you?" she began, and my instinct was recoil, and to revert to rudeness. I didn't want anyone to remember me.

"Grand," I tried to dismiss her. She wasn't giving up.

"I'm going home for first time in two years," she told me, "I am very pleased to be doing this."

"Good for you," was all I offered, but she was determined. On and on she went, about her job in catering in Dublin, and about how much she loved Ireland. And then came the questions, inevitably, about why I was visiting her country. It was at that point that I realised the opportunity, and began an elaborate fabrication on the hoof. I had done it before, creating an alias from thin air, and living it inside my head in order to support it again when questioned. It came rather naturally to me, which I often thought was a blessing, and an indication that I was not as decent a person as I wanted to be. Anyone who can lie like that has a dark element inside them.

I saw the Irish Daily Star in the pouch in front of her. "I work for them," I pointed to the paper. Her head followed my gaze to the seat in front.

"These people?" she gestured to the backs of the heads of the people in front.

"No, the newspaper. The Star."

"Oooh," she replied, interested. "What do you do for them?"

"I'm an investigator," I was suddenly bristling with bullshit. "I find people for journalists. Then the reporters go and interview them."

"And who are you looking for?" she inquired conspiratorially, lowering her voice as much as the racket from the jet engines would allow. I leaned in.

"A murderer," I replied, and let that sink in, hoping for awe. Hope misplaced.

"Well, you're coming to the correct country," she replied, "so many murderers I know."

This was not really what I had anticipated. She went quiet.

We sat for a long time, arms tucked in like chicken wings, as we puttered around with the unpacking and consumption of the tiny on-board meal. And then I struck. "I have pretty good expenses," I told her, "I could use your help."

"Not that type of woman," she hissed at me, immediately angry.

"No, no, that's not what I mean. Really, that's not what I meant."

I let her stew for a while, and sure enough, she eventually came back in better humour. "So, what *do* you mean?"

"A translator, to help me find the murderer."

"Oh," she sounded surprised. "Yes, I can do that."

The following day we met in the old town. I handed her a note, my best guess at spelling the name of Shannon's killer. It was hard to know how accurate it could possibly be, given that it had been gargled to me by a man in extreme pain, as I applied weight to a pressure point. With a rather knowing and superior air, the girl took my pencil and corrected it, and then began walking. I had no choice but to follow.

We entered a beautiful building on the edge of the old town, marble steps, open foyer, and severe-looking security guards. The woman at a central workstation appeared no less humourless, and greeted us with a stare rather than a smile. She said nothing, but the vacuum was filled by my bright companion, who managed to woo the woman out of her Soviet slumber. At one point, I actually saw her blink. Something got written on a piece of paper, and then we were at a computer terminal in another room, and then we were on the street again, walking alongside a tram. Vilnius struck me as city of two halves – the first a riddle of old cobbled streets and beautiful renaissance hotels and homes, the second a downtown area pleading for seediness and sex, and bling and big, black BMWs.

Eventually we arrived at an imposing, dilapidated construction. Our feet crunched in the snow as the girl stared up at the hundreds of broken windows above us. All around us were cracked streets and pavements falling into the gutters. An occasional fast food outlet stared onto the wasteland from which grew this Soviet bloc of a building. The girl eventually looked at me. "He's in there."

"Really? What is it?"

"Is a prison."

"Bollocks," I said in disappointment. She looked confused.

"You don't want a murderer in jail?"

"No. Yes. Of course. But, I wanted, you know, to get someone to interview him. To expose him."

"Then you're lucky," she said.

And then we were on the march again, and I was getting fed up with her lack of communication, and I tried to seek some answers. "Right, where are we going now and why am I lucky?"

"You are very, very lucky," she said. "He is to be at court today, and my uncle works at the court."

To be fair, that did strike me as very, very lucky, and a little unlucky, because a court didn't sound like an ideal place to snuff someone and get away with it. And my priority had to be to get away with it, or Isla would be left alone.

The girl was a whirlwind of energy. I could barely keep up with her as she wound me through the streets of Vilnius. We passed minimalist shops selling watches worth thousands, and markets for the poor which looked like little more than food banks. The place began to remind me of Moscow, where people appeared to be either destitute, or filthy, horribly, braggingly rich; the post-Soviet state of the nations which escaped. We eventually stopped on what looked like the main street, and she turned to face an imposing building with unnecessarily high doors, hung between gargantuan pillars.

"Wait here," she commanded, her bossiness betraying a desire to impress. I was on her turf, and she was evidently competent. As I stood there, I mused over how much time this woman had saved me. I reckon I can find just about anyone, just about anywhere. But it takes time. Where there are language barriers and where the Irish charm falls dead, as I suspected it would in this monosyllabic society, it could be a struggle. This woman was a bustling little dynamo, who seemed to have endless resourcefulness, and contacts, and I did, indeed, feel very, very lucky.

When she emerged, she was excited. She lowered her voice to a stage whisper. "He can get you in!"

I shook my head in wonder. Less than twenty-four hours after we'd landed, she had me a face-to-face. Of course, I had absolutely no idea what I would do with this opportunity, so I needed to think fast. "When's he due up?"

"What?"

"When will he be here?"

She looked at her watch for effect. "Three hours."

This was, frankly, not the best news. I thanked my new friend, and agreed to meet her later that day. She looked disappointed, but I couldn't really think of any gentle way to shake her, other than to offer to pay her for her time. She declined, which suggested to me that she was enjoying the excitement of it all as much as the prospect of being paid. And, of course, not taking the money kept her in the game for more fun later. This irritated me, as I didn't want to bring any trouble her way, or towards her uncle, and I needed that one-to-one with the killer.

The solution, as ever, presented itself as I haggled with the girl over her refusal to accept payment. An arse-about-face negotiation, I accept. I took a gamble, and asked her for guidance. "Do you know diabetes?"

"Of course," she said, moderately offended. "You need insulin?"

"Yes." What I needed was what came with it.

"Ok," she sighed, and we were off again, through the pretty part of town this time. Eventually we came to a cavernous chemist's, where she put out her hand to me for cash, and stomped off. I heard her barking orders at a fat woman in a white coat. They had an argument, the younger woman prevailed, and came back with a vial.

"Thank you," I said, "but I need the needle too, the syringe."

"Why you not bring with you?"

Good question. "Left it at the hotel."

"You must stay far away," was all she said as she turned and set-to with the pharmacist once more. We emerged victorious, and it was really time to part ways. I explained I would meet her at the court in two hours, and she agreed.

I'd spotted a metal works on the far side of the train tracks as we'd walked towards the jail. It was so close, yet so far away, as there did not appear to be any means of getting over the line. Eventually I gave up looking and skipped over the barrier, ran over the sleepers, and hurled myself at the fence on the far side. A ten-minute run took me to the gates of the factory, and the rapid click and buzz of welders told me I was in the correct place.

I worked quietly around the far side of the imposing shed, and found the delivery bay. Standing three barrels tall, in bright blue, with the universal skull symbols on them, was the stock of what I imagined to be hydrofluoric acid. It was a distant memory, but I recalled the warnings to stay away from this stuff when I'd trained at a rigging factory as a teenager. It's used to clean stainless steel, and we were told in no uncertain terms that a drop of the stuff on your skin could cause multiple organ failure. Because of the language of the writing, I had no idea if it was definitely what I wanted, but I had no time, and no other option. I broke the seal, and gingerly filled half a centimetre of the syringe, carefully replacing the needle cover.

Back in Vilnius centre I hunted for a gorilla pit. With only one hour left, I became a little desperate. At a slow jog, I covered about a mile, and eventually caught sight of a York sign above a door. Some brands are universal. I bounded upstairs and as I opened a door into a weights gym, every shaven, thick, robot head in the room rotated slowly towards me.

The next bit was tricky. I did my usual, "Do you speak English?" except I was speaking Russian, which was far from ideal. One powder monkey stepped forward and shrugged. "A little," he seemed to suggest. I then used sign language to explain what I needed, eventually miming an injection into the buttock, and he nodded, and called someone else over. I was motioned into a changing room, nervous that I was on shaky ground. I was confident enough however, that my build was sufficient to suggest I threw a few barbells about.

The second man rooted in his bag and produced a small but familiar-looking container, the type that some of my pals had used when bulking up post-training. I'd seen them shoot that shit into their arses, I'd seen the nose bleeds as they squatted and pressed, and gradually got too big to move quickly.

I paid the man and left. After a pause in a side street to add the steroids to the acid, I made for the court. I had no idea how long the syringe would last with all that stuff in it, and it felt warm to the touch.

My translator was waiting for me at the steps. She ushered me inside and took me to a man in uniform, who declined to greet me or to shake my outstretched hand. He opened a door and walked me down a series of corridors into a room, where he left me without uttering a single word. Suited me fine.

After an hour, the door opened and two alarmingly attired policemen came in. They had the whole outfit; batons, kneepads, elbow pads, padded baseball hats, stab jackets, handguns. I thought for a moment that I'd been screwed, and that I was about to be lifted. Then they hauled in a man about my size, and I knew I was looking at Shannon's killer.

He was fair, scarred, and snarling. This bastard looked like he craved conflict. He stared at me, goading me, confident that he could fight, despite the fact that his arms were secured behind his back. I opted for authority and nodded to the police officers to leave, which, amazingly, they did. It was just him and I, and at that point his attitude changed. His eyes narrowed and he began to regard me again, wondering who I was.

"You murdered my wife," I told him.

His pupils widened involuntarily, and I knew I had the right man. His mind plainly couldn't keep up with the confusion of seeing me there. Maybe it was my accent, maybe he had seen me around our village when I was home on leave. Regardless, he knew he was in the shit. I chose not to spend time with a dead man, stepped forward, and plunged the syringe into his thigh.

I stepped back as he screamed and kicked, hopeful that it would take hours, if not days, for him to die. Traces of steroids would not attract any attention in a prison. I was confident that a place like that would be awash with anabolic. I didn't care how they explained the acid. I suspected that they would ignore it, assuming they bothered with an autopsy at all.

Three hours later, and having spent all of my cash on a translator, her uncle, steroids, and a teddy for Isla, I was back at the airport, twitching for my flight to London to be called. If I could get through security at Heathrow, I was home and hosed. Another little bit of the re-build was complete.

Twelve

"Just fooking leave me alone."

I stared at the girl. She could not have been more than seventeen years old. She was swaying on top of soiled sheets, but in her head, she could well have been floating on clean, crisp clouds. I couldn't begin to imagine what had been pumped into her. She could barely sit, never mind stand. Her arms flailed around, as she grappled for purchase in the putrid air of the tiny room.

I didn't have to force entry. The door was wide open, and the smell of perfume and rubber tumbled down the stairwell. The charity woman had sent me to the address, a block of flats in Tallaght, Southwest Dublin. I had taken few precautions; I didn't intend to hurt anyone. Well, nobody who didn't deserve it, or who didn't try to hurt me first.

The charity woman had told me that there were at least three girls in the flat. I could only locate two, which was a bit of a worry, but also a waste of money, as I'd hired a people-carrier at the airport. If the intel had been accurate, I would have rented a smaller vehicle which would have been easier to park, and would have put a smaller dent in my dwindling finances.

This girl lunged to the side of her bed and popped back up, shuddering like a diving board, her head wobbling furiously. I stooped to pick her up and recoiled instantly when I caught sight of the needle in her hand.

"Wow wow now," I spluttered, "I'm here to help you, I'm not gonna hurt you, I'm not a punter. I'm here to take you home."

"Fook-a off yourself," she drawled. The poor kid was bombed beyond sense, and I was short on time.

"Who runs this place?"

She just stared at me. A voice came from behind.

"I do."

I turned to face a well-preserved fifty-something woman, glamorous perhaps, hair in an ornate weave on top of her painstakingly crafted façade. I stared at her for as long as I could, trying to get a fix, but wary of the kid with the pointy, infection-ridden weapon to my right.

The older one began to talk, confident and dismissive. "So, you're here to help them, are you?"

"What are you, like a madam or something?"

"I am an employer," she said. "And I also have an employer, and he will be back very soon."

God forgive me, but I had already considered flattening her by this point. Her selfishness made me cross, her willingness to treat these kids as tools. I knew the boss was a Romanian, but he'd obviously hired locally to give the whole grim escapade a native branding. The mutton was taking a phone from her bag, so I had to act.

I took a step to my left and curled her phone arm behind her back. There was a leather strap, not unlike a belt, attached to a radiator. It was alarmingly moist, and I bound her hands to the headboard of the bed. It's funny the things you think of; I rather imagined that this was not the first occasion on which someone had done that to the old pigeon. At least I hadn't hurt her, not badly. I lifted her phone, and realised that the contacts on it might be of use to the charity.

The woman was giving it loads by this stage. I muffled her by wrapping her head up nice and snug with semen-stained sheets, and rifled through her handbag. In it was a purse with at least a dozen neatly arranged credit cards. There was also a grisly and gnarled curl of fifty Euro notes, the proceeds of sex I assumed, and so due to the girls I'd been sent to rescue.

The kid needed help. Shannon would have hugged her, used reason and psychology and empathy. I slapped the syringe out of her hand, found a bag under the bed and bucked every piece of non-kinky clothing into it. Then I hoisted her over my shoulder and carried her down the stairwell to the car. I left her in the back, but she started shouting and giving out, and I wished I'd brought someone else with me. I locked her in, but she was bouncing about so much that the alarm went off. That wasn't acceptable, as someone would definitely call the Guards, and I still had another girl to get out of the flat. So, I took the first one back up with me again. It made me think about this story of the chicken and the fox and the boat, but I couldn't remember the solution.

At the top of the stairs I found the second girl, slightly older and moderately more sober, packed, and ready to go. Thank fuck," I said. The one over my shoulder was getting heavy-ish, and was still kicking. "Can you tell her to take it easy?"

To my amazement, the second girl formed a fist and hit the kid with such force that the wriggling stopped. I didn't really have time to reason that out. I just grunted and turned, and headed for the car. The aggressive one followed.

I put them both in the back and started driving. The fact that the violent one was behind me made me cross. This whole extraction had been full of mistakes, and I resolved to ensure that the next one would be properly planned and risk assessed. I began to wonder what had happened to me. I was getting sloppy, and too easily distracted.

As it turned out, breaking the girls out of the brothel was the least of my problems. I got to the Dublin airport, parked outside the shiny new departures terminal, and was immediately accosted by a Nazi parking attendant. He called a Garda when I told him to move aside. Then the bloody cop began to take an interest in the fact that I had what appeared to be two hookers in the back, and that one of them appeared to be heavily drugged. This was all incredibly inconvenient, so eventually I phoned the charity woman, who was supposed to be on the concourse awaiting our arrival.

Except she wasn't, which was something I would learn in this new business. Charity workers are brilliant people, but they are not altogether organised, and compared to the Navy, they're next to useless when it comes to the execution of even the simplest operation. Their passion crowds their practicality, and they argue over how things ought to be done, even in the midst of actually doing them. This was my first exposure to such silliness. I got on the phone.

Charity was late. It took a full fifteen minutes for her to arrive at the car, and to begin remonstrating with the cop. She, at least, had identification, and plane tickets for the girls.

But the Garda wanted to know who I was, and I didn't want anyone to know that. Then the charity woman wanted to know why one of the girls was half-conscious, and I wanted to know why any of that mattered in the circumstances. As far as I could see there were two issues – getting rid of the cop, and catching the flight.

Just to put a lid on proceedings, a massive white Mercedes pulled up and a shaven-headed thug emerged. He simply walked forward, grabbed girl number two by the upper arm, and led her away. I looked to the sky and wondered how, for the Love of God, I had ended up in this bloody situation, and looked to the Garda to intervene. The Garda looked terrified, so I spoke to him directly to try to shake him out of his frozen state.

"This is now a kidnap situation, and you are allowing two vulnerable women to be taken against their will. What do you intend to do about it?"

"I, I…. I'll radio for assistance."

"Well, I, I, will have to sort this bloody mess out while you panic, you prick," I said, and was forced, in full view of about twenty security cameras, to deal with the skinhead.

That bloke had balls. To try to take two women, on his own-ee-oh, in front of an ex-Marine, a cop, a woman, and a jobs-worth traffic attendant. As he came back to my hire-car to get the drugged kid, I walked around him and slashed his tyres on the passenger side. Of course, he got cross, and we had to face one another. The whole thing became quite convoluted and took a short age, but eventually I managed to come out on top, with a chewed ear and a possible broken nose. The charity woman hurried the girls inside.

As I drove away I caught the reflection of the Irish police arriving in force. I swerved into the Enterprise car-hire slot before they whizzed past in dynamic chase. The car was nearly returned before it had been rented, the same staff were on shift, and slightly baffled.

I'd hired it corporate, so the only ID that had been required was my license, which was a fake from my previous employment. I asked them to delete my stolen credit card details and handed over cash instead. I counted the notes I had intended to give to the trafficked girls. There was three grand there. I dropped an extra fifty euros on the counter.

"You might want to clean the backseat, wee drop of blood. Nothing serious," I told them, then walked into the Dublin thoroughfare, and jumped on the bus to Belfast.

Thirteen

I recalled that when I arrived in Jerusalem, there were guns everywhere. I was used to guns. I was even at ease around automatic weapons, but less so when they were slung over the shoulders of teenagers. Jerusalem was an eye-opener.

The market on Jaffa Road was a cacophony of colour. Fruit tumbled from the pitched stalls left and right, the produce of a land of milk and honey. This was a place where streams of children trotted along in single file, a rangy youth before and aft, each carrying a rifle.

There were arguments everywhere. Some might call them debates, but they were heated and heavy, and haggling seemed to be the local currency. Not once did I see shekels exchanged. At either end of the closed street were bitter-looking soldiers, young and conscripted, bored by their sedate posting. I had watched them wave their detector wands over the torsos of shoppers, in half-arsed fashion. It was useful to see that almost every building had a guard of some sort, and that weapons were not just tolerated, they were expected. What these people were scared of were suicide vests.

Money would have been a pain, but for the fact that Shannon had handed me a bundle as we left Gaza. I'd discarded my kit in Ashdod, bought some cheap clothes, and boarded a Sherut to Tel Aviv. That was an experience, a kind of shared mini-bus taxi affair, in which companionship was frowned upon. Suited me just fine.

Tel Aviv to Jerusalem was a similar arrangement. Nobody paid me any attention, until the driver insisted on an extra ten dollars to take me into the Arab section east of the city. He claimed Jews were afraid to go there, which was bollocks, as I soon discovered.

The American Colony Hotel was my only point of reference in the city. Some colleagues in the SBS had performed close protection there for a former prime minister, and had spoken fondly of its underground cavern. So that's where I told the driver to take me, but my mind changed instantly when I inquired about the cost of a room. I had no credit cards, no identification, and I would need more cash in the very near future. Not far around the corner I found the cheaper Christmas Hotel. There I got the first proper rest I'd had in a week. Still, the pause before sleep often brings anxiety, and I had plenty to worry about.

*****

I'd left my team to paddle west for a pick-up. They weren't too happy about it, and in the end demanded to know what was going on. I left the sergeant with a clear message to pass on to our CO; I'd had to do a deal to get the Op completed, and I would explain everything when I returned. Of course, I had no intention of explaining everything, but the operation had been successful, and I prayed for the wind to be at my back for the de-brief.

Against the odds, Ashdod had been a doddle. The mercy ship, as the campaigners had called it, was of little interest to the Israelis, and as such had been tied to a wall normally used by fishing boats. That harbour was poorly lit in comparison to the naval quays, which could have been seen from space. The effect was to plunge the surrounding water into almost complete darkness. Thus, we paddled in without detection, and boarded by climbing the Mercy Ship's seaward quarter.

The only tricky part was locating the explosives. One of my team stayed afloat, keeping the kayaks together with an eye on the blind side. Another lay in the lee of the starboard gunwale, keeping watch through the anchor eye. I needed the youngest man to come with me, as he had bomb disposal experience.

We combed through and cleared every inch of that stinking boat, which was packed to the teeth with tinned food and blankets. We'd been briefed that the Semtex, a plastic explosive, could be kept in just about anything because, as explosives go, it was pretty stable. To make the search more difficult, the stuff we were looking for was old. This meant that the markers, the colouring and the odour added to it since the 1990s, would be absent. It would be in a black wrapper, in oblong strips, and would have the texture of marzipan. I quite liked marzipan.

We were tired. The adrenaline charge from climbing aboard undetected quickly wore off. It struck me that the IRA might have managed to conceal the stuff in some tinned food, and so I began to scan the labels for a tell. A hopeless pursuit – there were thousands of cans on board.

I stood still, and began to rationalise the process that the arms smugglers must have gone through. Although resistant to heat and impact, I couldn't imagine anyone wanting to store that stuff close to the engine, to fuel, or in their own quarters. If the Semtex went up, it would take the boat to the bottom, so I couldn't see someone wanting to sleep beside it. I was looking for somewhere cold, and free from the clattering and banging of the waves, and away from the bunks.

I ruled out the wheelhouse, and opted to focus on a lower centre of gravity, where the movement of the sea would be less pronounced. I was gazing at the interior of the bilges, when my eye began to follow the steel piping around the hull. The tubes were painted the same colour as the walls. I knew one would carry cables, another seawater to cool the engine, and the third would take fresh water to the heads or toilet, and the galley. I started tapping them, seeking any disparity in the tone. As I got closer to a bulkhead, the sound dulled considerably. All three entered a timber boxed-off junction, and when I ripped the lid off, I found an extra pipe. It was fixed to the others. Unless one was counting how many tubes went through the bulkhead, and how many pipes were on the far side, it would have looked utterly normal.

We cut the pipe free and lifted it gently onto the table. The caps at either end were easily removed, and a slight tilt and gentle persuasion did the job. The pipe was packed, and it was clear that a lot more stuff had made it aboard than had been anticipated. It took another twenty minutes of pipe chasing to convince ourselves that there was no more, and we extracted.

We mustered one mile outside the harbour breakwater, and I fired up the phone and sent a message. While we waited, I broke the news to the others. The night was calming, but the mood turned rough.

"I need to go ashore again, I have unfinished business. I need you to get the explosives to the ship, and I'll be in touch as soon as I can."

That's when the argument began, and I had to pull rank. They weren't being disrespectful. Quite the opposite. They didn't want me to go alone, they wanted to know what was going on, and to help. But there was no option. In the middle of the discussion the phone lit up. We had orders.

"Your course is two-nine-zero. Sixteen nautical miles off shore is the RV. A Zodiac will pick you up," I told them.

The Sergeant led them reluctantly into the dark Med. I turned north, seeking a sheltered spot to come ashore, and sort myself out.

*****

The call to prayer woke me. A six-hour sleep had taken the edge off my unease. I stared out of the hotel window at the exodus of men streaming towards the Old City and the Mosque. There was something exciting about the uncertainty of what was happening around me. I was watching a Friday routine, as the shutters came down and the dust went up, and I decided to follow the sandals through the sandpit to Herod's Gate. I tried to put my worry aside and get on with what needed to be done. Acquiring a sense of place was as good a way to begin as any.

The smells of the old, walled city were dreadful, intense, and exotic in sequence. The stench of donkey dung at the perimeter was quickly replaced by sweetness and the must of age, and eventually, by burning incense sticks. The Muslims filtered towards the raised domes of their devotion, as nodding orthodox Jews prayed beneath the Western Wall, filling the cracks in the enormous stones with folded paper. It was quite a distraction, and it filled me with awe. My mind was drawn back to Iraq and Afghanistan. For the first time, I felt I was observing the genesis of the conflict which had drawn my pals and I into those wars, and so many of them into their graves.

I sat long into the evening, as Friday prayers became Shabbat, the occupation of the city rotating from one faith to another. Security tightened. The police were well-armoured.

I wanted to avoid being asked for ID I didn't possess, so I reluctantly sidled off into the night.

I knew that my status would shift to AWOL, and that someone would now be tracking my smartphone, regardless of whether or not I switched it off. So, it felt pointless not to use it to guide me through places familiar from the Bible stories of my childhood. From Mount Olive, I stared at the city. The light licked off the Golden Dome, the shadows cast from the church spires and synagogues and minarets. All reaching for God, each battling for space and primacy. To my left the dead were crammed, buried in the Promised Land at great personal expense. I thought of the cost of their repatriation, and then of the price paid by the families of my fellow bootnecks. Then I thought of the kids in Gaza, who'd had their futures destroyed by a rapist, before their existence had even properly begun. And I decided that there was nothing more important than life, and that for the deserving to live free, others might not live at all.

Fourteen

Dublin Bay

'"First comes dignity, Captain!"'

'"First comes discipline,"' screamed the epauleted Russian.

Not for the first time, I questioned the wisdom of my new career choice. I thought of Shannon, and what she would have made of what I was doing. My eyes tightened and my lips thinned at the reflection.

So I died, you left the navy, and jumped straight into a shit fight? Well done Sam, that's just what Isla needs.

I could hear her as clearly as if she were on the ship with me.

"Take me to the crew, Captain!"

I looked on in amazement at the little Dubliner as he squared up to the ship's skipper. At five-foot-seven, he was dinky in comparison, but this man appeared to know no fear.

No," replied the officer, incredulous. "You are not welcome on this ship, you must leave."

Even after years in the Marines, the Special Forces, and hauling myself around harbours and oceans, I shared a little of the Captain's surprise that we had made it onto his bridge. His ship was still at sea, after all. This was not what I had expected.

Frankly, I'd been reluctant to answer when Charity called with another job. The Dublin airport debacle had left me feeling exposed. Nobody had come looking for me though, and the wrestling match hadn't made the news or social media. Still, my face was now on record somewhere, and those CCTV images made me want to stay out of Dublin for a while. Then the charity woman mentioned ships, and suddenly, I was interested.

All I had been told was that a man who dealt with exploited seafarers would meet me at the gates to Dublin Port. I took the bus, and found the bloke sitting in his car, talking on a Bluetooth speakerphone. I knocked the window and he beckoned me into the passenger seat, and then I enjoyed five minutes of his colourful conversation. Basically, he was trying to persuade some foreign bloke to take on his penalty points for speeding on his motorbike. It was a fun listen.

"If I get any more, I'll lose my license," he explained to me. "Yer man won't care. He's leaving in a few weeks anyway, back to Poland," was the only elaboration I got. "Fran," he said, and leaned over to shake my hand.

"Sam," I replied.

"So, brother, you've been with the Brits, have you?"

Normally this would have put me on notice; so many people in Ireland are inherently hostile to the U.K.'s armed forces. Yet it was immediately obvious that this wee man was taking the piss.

"Yes," was all I said, and we settled in, as if we'd known each other forever. He explained the job. A ship full of Filipinos, under a flag of convenience, was heading for the port. It was run by a Russian shipping agency, and Fran had issues with the poor treatment of the ratings, the blue-collar grafters, aboard. I had questions.

"How do you know about this?"

"SMS my friend, text message, the wonders of technology." He held up his phone, and shook it with a roguish grin, before tapping away and reading from the screen.

"Dear Mr Fran," he began, "from MV Gallant at anchor in Fort Lauderdale. We due Dublin in six week. Please help. No good on ship. No pay many day. No permitted to leave ship. Many crew Philippines. Not return home in year. Please help us."

"Seriously?" I asked.

"Modern slavery brother, but hidden," he said, dramatically. I liked him from the outset. "Every port has a mission to seafarers, and every mission has a little booklet. And my number, brother, is in the booklet."

I knew of the missions, religious organisations designed to cater to the spiritual needs of those in peril on the seas. I'd seen the booklets too, but I'd never read one. "Why your number?" I asked.

"I'm the rep for the ITF, the International Transport Federation."

"A trade union?"

"Exactly brother, but you wouldn't know anything about that, would you? You are not allowed to organize, being at her Majesty's Service wha?" He chuckled away.

We drove into the port, and he waved merrily at scowling stevedores, who obviously knew him. I started to get a sense of why he needed me. "You don't seem to be too popular around here," I said.

"They love me really," said Fran, his cheery disposition masking a serious determination. "They just get pissed off when I arrest a ship, and their shift runs over."

"You can arrest a ship?"

"I can brother, under maritime law, and that's what you and me are going to get up to today."

That sounded like more fun than trailing hookers out of disease-ridden flats. These were the type of seamen I was used to. As we entered an office, a man who turned out to be the harbour master dropped his head into his hands in despair. "Ah Fran man, not again, I told the wife I'd be home to watch the young one."

"Well, comrade, with cooperation and good will towards your fellow human beings, we'll be out of your way in a jiffy."

"What is it Fran?" asked the harbour master.

"A big shiny red ship is sitting on the edge of Dublin bay. Belize flag, Russian Captain, fifteen Filipinos on board. No pay for two months. No agreement, no right to leave. I want them unionised, and paid, or allowed ashore for repatriation."

"Ah look," the harbourmaster shook his head. "Why today? I'm about to go on me holidays. Could you not have come tomorrow?"

"I'll do you a deal," said Fran. "I'll not arrest the ship at the quay, if you can get me out there to sort it out. And then, if I can get an agreement and the men paid, your men can unload it and send it on its merry way."

"And if there's no agreement?"

"Then I'll arrest it at sea, and you'll have the dock clear for the next ship that comes along. But what I'm suggesting leaves you with a chance to get home before dinner."

The harbour master stared at Fran for a few moments, then got on a radio and told the crew of the pilot boat to free up a seat.

"Two," said Fran.

"Who's your pal?" asked the Harbourmaster, tipping his head to the side, meaning me.

"This is a brother in arms," said Fran, and winked at me.

Every major port has a pilot. They board incoming cargo and container ships to make sure that captains unfamiliar with the harbour don't run aground, and snarl up shipping traffic for days. Ports make money on the speed of a turnaround. From the dockers, or stevedores who unload the holds and steel containers, to the customs officers and administrators, there is an urgency to get a ship in and out, as quickly as possible.

The pilot boat hammered through the waves, rather than over them, and I felt happy to be back on the water. As we neared the ship, a tiny rope ladder was flung over the side, and for the first time I saw concern in the little Dubliner's eyes. I was in my element. He stood on the foredeck as the pilot boat leapt and plunged, his hands out for balance, as if he was riding a skateboard for the first time.

As a wave crest neared, I swept out and grabbed the ladder with one arm, and his shoulder with the other, and hefted him onto the first rung. After that he had no choice, and was up and away like a mortar out of a tube. I followed fast and he treated me to a heel on the forehead as we neared the top. On board he was elated, and ready to rumble. A bulky Russian met us at the top, complete with clipboard. "Pilot yes?"

"Yes, Pilot," Fran lied. "Take me to the bridge."

The Russian complied, and off we went, up the steep steps, winding through the ship, and eventually into a modern, well-provisioned command room. Fran rather hit the ground running. "Captain, you're a cunt," he said, which took *me* aback, never mind the man to whom it was directed.

"Who are you?" asked the wide-eyed skipper. Fran introduced himself, and the Captain realised he'd been rumbled.

"Get off my ship, get off, you have no rights here!" he screamed.

Obviously, this was not a new thing on cargo vessels, Fran must have pulled this stunt before. "I have every right, as you well know, Captain," Fran began in his florid, eloquent way.

He then reeled off some ancient law of the sea. I began to enjoy myself, watching this little rascal's performance. He was animated, passionate, committed, and enormously funny. "Sixty days at sea, no pay captain! You have one man on board who hasn't been allowed ashore for one year, Captain. One year!"

"No!" roared the Russian. "We pay them."

"A dollar a day, Captain. Would you work for a dollar a day?"

"This is what they sign up for," said the Captain.

"Well, where are the contracts, Captain?" Fran shouted back, plainly convinced that contracts would not be forthcoming.

The ding-dong went on for about fifteen minutes, during which time the First Officer came up and, although I have no Russian, basically suggested to the Captain that we ought to be thrown overboard. This, I felt, was part of my role, so I stepped between the arguing men and the First Officer, and adopted an expression which made it clear that he was to back off. Like a dog scolded, he retreated.

The Captain radioed ashore, and the Harbour Master refused permission to dock until "matters had been resolved." His second call was to his shipping agency employer, and after much discussion, he agreed to take us to the crew. In the bowels of the ship we came across ten small, frightened Filipinos in jump suits. The Captain stood in the doorway, imposing his presence, until Fran rounded on him. "Fuck off Captain," he said, "or you will not get to unload this ship all week."

Interestingly, the unloading of the cargo appeared to be the most pressing matter, and so the Captain withdrew. Fran got to work.

"Who speaks English?" To my surprise, all the men raised their hands. "Excellent," said Fran. "Who texted me?" A rather timid little man raised his paw, and the others looked at him with astonishment.

"I did not know you would come," said the man.

"Well, here I am, brother, and if you all stick together, we can get this sorted out. More pay, and off the boat, and home to your families. But you need to stay together. Do you understand?"

The body language was fascinating. Clearly, they were afraid, some more than others. It was not at all clear, however, that they were of one mind. Fran picked out one man who had begun to glower at the sailor who had made the contact.

"What's your problem? Are you scared of the Captain? Don't you want to be paid a fair wage?"

This larger man was exposed, and I realized what a master of negotiation Fran was. Pick the big one in a fight, and the rest will buckle.

"Aaaah, is problem for me," he spluttered. "I need monies for sending home."

"How much do you send home, Brother?" Fran softened.

"Maybe... maybe. Eh, thirty dollars every month."

"My friend," said Fran, "you should be earning thirty dollars every day. Lookit, you should be earning sixty dollars a day, but we are people of the world, and we know you were signed up in Manilla, where exploitation is a national sport."

"They have our sea books," said the man.

"If you work as one and refuse to do your jobs and unload this ship, I can get you thirty dollars a day. You can join the union, and we can get your sea books, and you can all get off this ship."

The men looked sceptical. Without the sea books, they could not work again. I knew enough about commercial shipping to work out that the papers were their license to operate. I also wondered where a breach of contract would leave them, with regard to their hiring agent back in the Philippines.

Fran lowered his tone, and began to persuade and coax them towards trusting him, and then he left them to discuss the options amongst themselves. Outside, the Captain and First Officer were trying to eavesdrop, but the hum of the ship made that virtually impossible. They demanded to know which of the crew had called Fran. He swore at them with utter contempt, and suggested to them that I was some sort of trained assassin, who would slaughter them in their sleep if they so much as scolded the crew. It was all great craic.

Eventually, Fran returned to the mess, and withdrew a laptop and papers. He signed up all the men to union membership. He made call after call, booked flights and a mini-bus, and allowed the men to prepare to dock the ship. The pilot boat returned with the real pilot on board, and the vessel tied up to the quay. The Captain signed the agreements, and I watched with incredulity as he withdrew hundreds of thousands of dollars from the ship's safe, and began to count out the cash.

With each man paid, and their sea books released, Fran marched them off the ship and they were whisked off to the airport. The whole thing had taken less than five hours. Fran and I went drinking, and arose the next day to hear that the ship's name had been changed, a new crew had been flown in, and the agreements torn up.

"Ah well, fuck it anyway," said Fran. He was visibly distressed at the thought of more seafarers being treated badly. He was a mischievous little man, but his heart was in the right place.

He sighed. "I'll get that ship next time it comes to Ireland, and we'll do it all over again."

So, Charlie had a new client, and I started to see a way through financially, for the first time in ages.

Fifteen

It was as if a weight had been lifted. My ability to provide for Isla had been a nagging worry; not a priority, but it did invade my head at times. I remembered how Shannon had juggled to devote time to my re-building. She somehow managed to clear the decks during my periods of leave. My intention was to do the same for Isla when she needed it. And she would need it.

I knew that whatever job I settled on, enormous flexibility would be required. It felt like my little service, "Charlie," would give me just that. Short bursts of work, plenty of time to be there for my kid. Until I met Fran and the woman I would learn to call Charity, I'd had no real idea where I would fit in civilian society.

The main issue was how we were living. The boat was brilliant. Isla seemed to love the adventure and freedom of it. It also brought constant proximity, and that helped our recovery. I did worry that we would become too dependent upon one another, and that she would become accustomed to my company, rather than that of friends her own age. But we weren't ready to return to land.

I think I probably used our circumstances to prolong life at sea. I justified my nomadic inclinations by telling myself that it was useful to keep moving. The pressing issue was security. Isla needed it, and until the intruder stepped aboard, we largely had it, cruising the coast and settling somewhere different almost every evening.

She needed it because we had not yet confronted her mother's death. For a long time, I just didn't know how. There were times while roaming an island or on a beach, when I nearly opened the wound. The temptation was to try to disinfect it, so that when it was stitched up again, it might heal. It felt as though infection could set in at any time, but that the treatment could only be performed in a fresh, clean surrounding.

We were rowing in the dinghy, the day I finally dropped it. She was behind me as I hauled on the oars. She looked ahead, telling me when I was veering off course. We were going to lift a lobster pot, and she had the binoculars and a bucket, in case we got lucky. "Isla," I began.

"You're not going very straight Daddy."

"Isla, we need to talk about Mammy."

"Ok," she said, brightly.

Ok, I thought. Keep her steady. "We need to talk about the day she died darling," I said.

"Oh-wuh," she replied, like she did when I told her it was bedtime. It was as if she knew it was inevitable, but she wanted to delay it as long as possible.

"We have to, wee love, it's important."

"Why?"

Good question.

"Cos it's not good to have that memory in your head, and not let it out."

"Like the memories in your head?" she asked.

"What do you mean?"

"Mam said you have bad memories in your head. That's why we had to leave you alone sometimes. She said that to me. She really did."

I could hear Shannon saying it "Yes, wee lamb, like that. You need to get those bad memories out of your head so they can stay out as much as possible."

"I don't really want to talk about it," she replied, to my astonishment. It was such a grown-up sentence for a five-year-old. Perhaps it was inspired by too much T.V.; perhaps she had been thinking about it.

"We have to, wee darlin'. It'll be ok though, I'll mind you."

"Oh-wuh," she said again, and then adopted distraction tactics. "I can see the buoy!" she shouted.

"We'll lift the pots in a minute, Isla. First, we just need to talk about that night, ok?"

"Oh-kaay," she relented. We were still not looking at one another, which perhaps helped.

"Can you tell me what happened?"

"I already told everyone, Daddy!" she protested.

She meant the police, I assumed, which was before I had got back from Bastion. I knew she hadn't spoken to my folks, or Shannon's. "One more time, Isla. Please."

"The man cutted Mammy," she puffed a big breath out.

"Do you know why he did that, Isla?" I asked softly.

"Cos Mammy got mad with him, cos he nearly ran me over on my bike."

"Where darlin, where did he nearly run you over?"

"On the wheel, it was all bended over and broken."

"I know darlin', I mean where did it happen?"

"On the wheel daddy, I told you."

I gave up on that line of inquiry. "Ok, when did it happen, Isla?"

"When me and Mammy were going for ice cream. I had my helmet on, Daddy," she said defensively.

"I know you did, darlin'," I said, trying to soothe her. "What did Mammy say?"

"She said he was full up of beer," Isla said, which was the first time I had heard that.

"Did she?"

"She shouted at his car and he was smoking out the window."

I thought for a moment, the fog lifting a little. "What happened then?"

"He stopped the car and said really bad words to Mammy, and I shouted, "Don't you say that to my MAM," and then Mammy told me to be quiet and she had a cross time with him.""

"Were they close together?"

"No," said Isla, as she trailed off. "We just went home."

"What happened then?"

"I think Mammy called the police."

I knew this from the crime log, and from the phone record. The solicitor had even obtained the call and played it to me. I listened to an agitated Shannon react with measured incredulity, as she was told that there was no squad car available. She gave the license plate number, the man's address, and full details of the incident, but it was clear that nothing would be done. That's why she had gone for the nuclear option.

"What did Mammy do then?"

"She put me in the back of the car and we went to the man's house."

The house of horrors, built by the factory owner to house his staff, who then paid him rent.

"Ok, and what did she do at the house?"

"She didn't press the doorbell or anything. She just went inside and left me in the car seat." Isla sounded shocked, even now.

"How long was she in the house?"

"Superfast," said Isla.

"She came back out straight away?"

"Uh-huh," she said. "Daddy, you need to go over this way." She tapped my left shoulder.

I kept rowing slowly. "What do you think happened in the house?" I asked.

"She took away the bad man's car keys so he couldn't drive when he was full up of beer," said Isla.

"Did she?" This came as a total revelation to me.

"Yes," Isla said, in a perky tone, pleased that she was being helpful.

"How do you know?" I asked.

"'Cos I saw the keys," she said.

"But, the police never found any keys," I said aloud.

She went silent.

Suddenly everything started to become clear. I wished, and wished, and wished I could go back twenty minutes. I wished I had never started the conversation.

I stopped rowing. Isla sat silently, her back to mine. I looked over the side of the dinghy, at our reflections. Her head fell forward.

"That's why the man came with the knife," she said.

I closed my eyes. I knew what was coming next.

"He shouted at Mammy to give him the keys," her voice began to break.

"But you were in bed, weren't you darlin'?"

"I heard the man shouting at Mammy."

"What was he saying?"

"He was saying, 'Where are the keys, you fucking bitch.'"

There is a shockwave associated with hearing a child swear, even if it is to repeat the words of an adult. I felt sick.

"What did Mammy say?"

Silence.

I tried again. "What did Mammy say, wee love?"

"I don't know. I don't know!" she said, her little voice rising in tempo and distress.

We were in it now. I knew in my heart what had happened. I knew she had been carrying it around for months, and I decided it was time to purge it. "Did you get up out of bed?"

"Yes daddy."

"Why?" I asked, but I already knew the answer.

"'Cos I knew where the keys were," she began to sob, deep, gulping cries.

I dropped the oars. One fell into the water, as I turned to hug her. I gathered her up onto my lap and wrapped her in tight. Her tears soaked into my shirt. I willed the pain out of her, and into me.

"I hided the keys in my bag," she said.

It felt, to her, like an admission to a bold act. To me, it felt like a necessary pain which needed out, needed nailed, and the blame directed where it was due.

"That man was a bad man, Isla." I placed her brow to mine, trying to look into her eyes.

"But..."

I interrupted her. "Isla, that man was a bad man. He came to hurt Mammy and it didn't matter if he found his keys or not," I said.

"No, Daddy!" she pleaded now, "He just wanted his keys and Mammy couldn't find his keys cos I hided them," she said, pushing back from me. "Mammy looked everywhere," she opened her hands, eyes now wide open in exclamation.

"Mammy didn't want the bad man to have the keys," I said.

"She did Daddy, cos the man had a big knife," she said.

I held her back into me for a while. "You saw what he did, didn't you?"

"Mmmm hmmm."

"Did the man say anything after hurted Mammy?"

"He was laughing," she sobbed, "and he went 'aaaghhh!' to scare me and he did scare me," she said.

I thought of the fucker writhing in a cell in Vilnius, and hoped it had taken days of roaring anguish.

"Did Mammy say anything to you?" I asked, eventually.

"She was screaming at the man to get out, get out, get away from me, get out."

We just rocked backwards and forwards for a while.

"I gave Mammy a hug and then I got the plasters. But she died."

We cried together, for a short age, until the sun fell and the chill came. We were wrapped up, two sets of demons working hard inside each of our heads.

"Isla," I said eventually.

"Yes, Daddy," she said.

"You did the right thing, wee lamb. Mammy didn't want that bad man to find his keys. She was just pretending to look for them. She wouldn't want that man to drive with beer in him, cos he could have hurt another wee girl, and Mammy wouldn't have wanted that."

I could feel her thinking, and then she nodded into my chest.

"You did the right thing, Isla," I said. "Mammy was very proud of you."

"How do you know?"

"'Cos I'm your daddy and I know stuff, wee lamb. I know. Sometimes I can hear Mammy talking to me."

"So can I," she said.

"I can hear her laughing," I said, not at all sure whether such confessions were useful or harmful.

"Me too," she said.

"Mammy is always with us," I told her, and with that a white dandelion blossom blew across the boat and stuck to the Velcro on her lifejacket. She looked up at me, and smiled, then stroked it, and rested again. As if there was the dawning of some sort of peace in her heart.

*****

Six months passed, and Isla adjusted. I can't say that she recovered – I'm absolutely sure that she never will. Her sleeping improved, and gradually, when enraptured by the discoveries of life, as any five-year-old ought to be, her smiles, sparingly, returned. Three nights out of four she would sleep in her own cabin. I always offered her the option to bunk in with me, but after a while she seemed to prefer her own peace. That pleased me, of course, but it also left a kind of void.

Back then I had no time to address my own head issues. For weeks, I was little more than a coffee-fuelled, vacant carcass, attentive only to Isla, and ignorant of all else. I filled my time with jobs; sanding, varnishing, servicing the engine, setting the rig. The boat was in beautiful shape, but my mind was a mess.

As Isla edged towards contentment, I found my head occupied by a hostile force, distorted by noise. I remember exactly when it began. I was standing on the cross trees of the mast, twenty feet up and working on something which was working just fine. Perhaps it was the view from up there that did it, like an observation post from high ground, over the plains of Afghanistan. I received a radio transmission in my head, and I damn nearly fell backwards onto the deck below.

"Urgent Casi-vac required," the squelch and the break-up were unmistakable, the volume painful. I swiped at my ear to remove an earpiece that wasn't there. It struck from nowhere. I had not a thought in my head at that moment about Helmand, or the Corps, or anything really. It was like a cupped hand had hit me hard on the side of the head, and shattered my eardrum. I hugged the mast, slid to the spreaders, and sat still for a very long time. Only Isla' calls shook me from what was becoming a consuming fear.

I concentrated on other things, and tried to distract my mind, as well as my body. I began to take Isla onto new islands. I'd leave her at the highest point, where she could see me and I could see her. Then I'd run around the shore. I belted hard and fast, to the point of puking. She became confused by my vomiting. I told her it was just part of training for muscles. Then I'd force myself into a hundred push-ups, while she tried to count for me. She stumbled after thirty, but we got there eventually.

I think my mind softened as my body hardened. I wanted the alertness to subside when I was alone with Isla. I wanted the pain endured in the Afghan mountains to clear from my peripheral vision. At times, it felt that if I looked anywhere other than straight ahead, the horror would be waiting for me on the edges. I kept seeing dust, and the charring on the faces of those with whom I had served. The torn lips, the exposed teeth. Men trying to talk through their disfigured faces, unaware of their permanent contortion, or their imminent death. The most frustrating dream was the one in which I was helpless to do any good. The inability to stem the flow of rich, warm blood into the arid earth of a land where no man had any business to be. I think most of it stemmed from what became the longest day of my life.

I hadn't heard the noise at first. The dust went up like water out of a blowhole, straight and true. I was fifty feet away, and the sound took minutes to break into my head. We were patrolling between two hills, in a line, on our way to deal with two Taliban touts who'd been reporting on our movements for days. Back at the OP, our men scanned the mobile phone signals for Intel. If we could confirm that the two men were sending information to the enemy, we could remove them. Otherwise, we had to let them carry on.

We knew that tracking these men was dangerous, that they could deliberately draw us into fire. My call – carry on regardless. Too many of my men had been shot, my patience with our rules of engagement was exhausted, and I wanted some peace. We got anything but.

"Get the doc, get the doc!"

The shouting was mine, but I didn't feel as though I was talking. I ran forward, and crouched by our lead man, directing others to drop and stop. Two were directed to higher ground, to secure cover for what would be an extraction of the casualty. From then on, it was like a movie. I kneeled in silence, unable to comprehend what was happening. Plume after plume erupted. The noise just wasn't there. I don't understand why. I watched in utter silence as mines exploded and threw bits of four more marines into the air.

"Nobody move! Nobody move!" Casi-vac said immediately. "Doc, no movement. Triage from where you stand, tell me what's needed."

How I didn't die that day is a mystery. The doc hurled me his bag, and within minutes we were out of morphine. I found it remarkably easy to screen out the screaming, as I concentrated on our medic's instructions, and moved between my men. I packed their wounds, and tightened the tourniquets as they writhed in agony. Then we sat in the sun and waited. It took all day, as we burned and blistered in the dirt. On the ridgeline around us we could see friendlies' skyline, keeping us covered from secondary attack. I remember wishing it, craving the approach of a Taliban wave. Part of me felt we should all perish in that valley.

When the Casualty Evacuation helos did eventually arrive, they ignored every warning. Their airmen appeared with stretchers and stood in the middle of that minefield, and triggered nothing. One by one my men were taken into the sky, all beyond mending. Two died on the way back to Bastion. Two never walked again, one will never utter another word. I got a medal, which would later save me from dishonourable discharge, but I felt I should have got killed.

*****

Jobs came in pretty regularly. The charity woman seemed to have quite a network. I saw parts of Ireland I had never even heard of, as I marauded around, plucking women from apartments, flats, houses and even caravans.

I was careful, always, but I knew the risk was increasing. As my confidence rose, there was the potential to unpick that good work. At Dublin Airport, I knew that I had been seen on CCTV, and there were likely other occasions when I hadn't clocked a camera. I began using an old phone, a Nokia, as my point of contact, which was comparatively safe. But it was still a cellular device and therefore traceable. I found credit cards as I went, and used them to secure hire vehicles. Which was fine, but the cops would eventually catch up with me. All of that had to stop.

The charity woman was receptive to my concerns, and had a ready solution in the form of her twin sister. The twin was some sort of tech guru, who worked for one of the multi-nationals which had flooded Dublin in recent years. I didn't ask too much. I was broadly familiar with the bond and trust between such siblings, so I let her get on with it.

In the end, I was issued a dual-sim smartphone, one for the UK, one for Ireland. I was shown an app on it, which would alert me every time an inquiry was made on a site she had set up on the dark web. The only people who could access that website were those who typed in the exact, complicated URL. It could not be searched for on Google, or any other engine. I tried, and failed. When I opened the site, its message was suitably oblique.

"This is Charlie. For inquiries, leave your details, we will be in touch."

Charlie, as a name, had resonance. When I was forced to think of a name for my business, I thought of Shannon. That thought took me to a bombed beach in Gaza, and the operation that had taken me there. And our call sign on that operation was simple. It was Charlie.

The app on the phone did not provide a banner or an alert. I had to swipe through and check for any new messages. Then I would log in, and retrieve the details. I kept it at a dead drop in Belfast, and took to moving around a lot before I would make contact, sometimes up to one hundred miles. I used the app to make calls, in an attempt to mask the mobile signals, which I knew were exceptionally vulnerable to interception.

Around that time, I was coming around to the view, poked at by my parents, that Isla should start going to school. She was getting stronger, and too much time in my company, especially when my head was so melted, was probably not good. I was just about to leave the phone at the dead drop one morning when I decided the time had come. I fired it up and began searching for enrolment information. I will always remember casually consulting the app. The message meant little at the time. It was just a name, a request for contact, and a number. We needed to get food in, so I decided to make the call from a supermarket.

At Tesco, I pulled up as far from the doors and cameras as possible, and tapped the number. The accent of the man who answered was unmistakably Dublin, and like many from that city, he was talkative and inquisitive. Reining him in before he said too much, we agreed to meet at the gates of the Castle in three hours. This seemed to surprise the man, but I was determined not to allow him too much prep time, in case he was a spook, or a cop.

I called my folks and told them, yet again, that a job had come in, and arranged for Isla to sleep over. The drive ahead of me would take just over an hour. It was exciting in its own way. This was, after all, my first client other than Charity or Fran. I was a little apprehensive, and a lot suspicious. With good reason, as it turned out.

Sixteen

Jerusalem

I hadn't really expected men to hold hands. Jerusalem was an eye-opener for me. It wasn't like a normal deployment, where I was surrounded by my own team or unit. In Jerusalem, I was on a one-man mission, a private engagement, inspired by an exchange with a woman I barely knew. This gave me time to inhale the inland air, the strange scents, and to watch the waft and wane of life as it swept, in force, through the streets of that city. Ordinarily my time would have been consumed with briefings and preparation, but I had no kit to check, and no maps to consult. All I had was a name, and an ill-defined outcome to achieve.

Prejudice, preconception, and all manner of undesirable emotions made themselves known to me during that week. I had always considered myself pretty liberal, despite having spent my service surrounded, in political terms, by those to the right of the right. I felt that people ought to be left alone, unless they were causing others harm or hassle. As rules went, mine felt simple and straightforward. I wasn't aware of any personal hang-ups in terms of race, religion, or romantic inclination. My faith was my own business, and I harboured a suspicion that any person who lived a decent and generous life would find their way to God. Jerusalem though, challenged my ideas of myself, and not in a good way.

I'd grown up in Northern Ireland during the conflict, so the notion that people could be hostile towards others without even knowing them wasn't particularly new. Israel and Palestine though, were on a whole different level. I understand it better now, but I shall never understand it properly.

I felt drawn to the dustier, dirtier, eastern quarter of the city. There seemed to be less order, more madness, and greater animation in speech and mannerism. I found it soothing, friendly and familiar, although I'm not sure why. While eating a Falafel pita on a bench by the old city's ancient walls, a man came and pissed against the stones, less than a foot from my head.

The more cosmopolitan part of Jerusalem was an austere affair. You might get a handshake, but you were unlikely to receive a smile. Everybody seemed to feel under siege, something I, at least, was used to. All inhabitants appeared to be convinced that without a hard stance, they'd be on the cusp of losing all that they had worked for.

I tailed my man for two days, from the U.N. building to his home, from his home to a café, from the café to work. Despite the absence of evidence, I never really questioned my presence there. I trusted Shannon, although I barely knew her. We'd said very little to one another, yet she'd taken up residence in my head, and nestled in between the hard rocks of my heart. I didn't feel that I needed confirmation of the man's paedophilic inclinations. But I got it anyway.

He meandered irritatingly around a few bars, sipping feminine-looking drinks from delicate little glasses. This made him a tough tail. I would never normally follow someone alone; I'd be part of a team that would rotate and swap, taking control of the mark. We would keep everyone on the net, the radio comms up-to-date on every little detail, like a stream of consciousness. In Jerusalem though, I had no radio, no team, and looking back on it now, no rational thought. If I had followed my training, I would have exploited the woman I'd met in Gaza, and got out when the operation was completed. Perhaps my new target wasn't the only one driven by his desires.

Eventually he went to a small, independent cinema. I waited a few hundred metres away, but not before I checked out what was showing. It was a film for the U.K.'s Channel Four, about the death of a cameraman who had been filming in Gaza. At least my target's cover was consistent.

Inside there was a reception, with drinks, glad-handing, and air kisses, so I waited outside until it all ended. Eventually, hugs complete and on his own, he made a mobile phone call. He then paced aimlessly for a few minutes, before climbing slowly up a steep footpath to higher ground, and towards a heath. As dusk fell it became easier to track him. His pace slowed when he entered an ornately paved public area. I checked my phone for location, the Lion's Fountain, close to Hebron Road. Bushes and trees surrounded it, but through gaps in the foliage the view of the city's lights was impressive. I didn't realise what the place was until it was too late.

I lost him in the space of a few seconds. I began to hunt, a little too desperately in hindsight, given that I knew where he lived and worked, and could have picked him up the next day. But I was scared that he may have made me, so I speeded up and would have betrayed myself, had it not been for an orthodox Jew, and a man in a leather jacket. The Jewish man was standing, loitering, for no reason. The man in the leather jacket was looking at me, eager. Even in the half-light, I could make out his excitement, although it wasn't pronounced enough to cast much of a shadow.

There are some areas of life in which I am considerably slow. The Marines gave me skills few others possessed, but immersion in military life leaves enormous gaps in ordinary knowledge, and every-day experience. It took this man to beckon me towards the bushes for the penny to finally drop. I was being cruised.

I ignored the amorous man in the leather jacket and began to hunt through the hedges in pursuit of my mark. Moments later I heard the final grunts of his pleasure, and in the gloom, I saw the face of a boy rising, as he clutched his trousers and secured them at the waist. They'd made enough noise to conceal my arrival, and as the kid was being paid, I had all the knowledge I needed. I looked at the boy; he was no older than twelve. The man I was interested in left the heath onto the main street, and walked at a heightened pace back towards his home. I decided to get there first.

Seventeen

Dublin

My plan had been to watch for the new client's arrival, to gather a sense of the man, before revealing myself. I stood on the concourse of Dublin's Heuston station, and waited and watched, but he beat me to it. My eyes fell upon him long after his found me. He had hunted me out.

Perhaps it was no great achievement, on his part. At just under six feet, I'm not particularly tall, but if I stand outside a pub, people automatically assume I am the bouncer. Younger ones nod to me with a kind of sheepish deference. If I make my way through a crowd, it parts. I look a little menacing when I'm thinking; Shannon called it my "Halloween face," and I bulk up quickly if I'm training. I hadn't thrown weights around since I'd left the service; at forty years old, it seemed pointless to maintain excess muscle that I wouldn't need outside the Marines. Besides, feeding muscle with protein is expensive. But I did work my own mass, chin-ups, press-ups, and squats, so my shoulders were stacked and my posture probably betrayed me a little. That and the fact that I have always shaved my head, but seldom my chin, and I look like what I am; a salty, over-exposed sailor with cracks round my cheeks and eyes, hands like paddles, and the arms of a wrestler. I am not pretty, and I dress only for practicality. On reflection my shell jacket, heavy denims and cross-trainers meant that I could not have looked more like a de-mobbed Marine, if I'd tried.

Anyway, this potential client evidently knew who I was, and he bore through me with intensity. Even at two hundred yards, he was an unnerving presence, mentally rather than physically, and he unsettled me from start to finish. He took me to a tall Georgian Terrace, and we creaked up old timber stairs to a small room. It was warm, and in contrast to the rest of the building, soothing and pleasant. The conversation, was not.

"I think you understand evil," was his opening gambit. I remained mute, and immediately shuttered up, convinced that he was going to try to shock me. Despite my preparation, he succeeded. "I have a job for you, if you have the balls for it."

That irritated me. I don't feel that I need to have my courage tested, and I don't like goading. It's kids' stuff, and it's pointless. This fella wanted to reverse the arrangement, to lock me in. I didn't want to be locked in to anything. I'd spent seventeen years locked in to the Navy, and now I was sailing free, working when I wished. I stayed silent and let him plod through his little pantomime.

"I was once a clinical psychologist," he said. "Now, I look after the afflicted and tend to their wounds," he tapped his temple. I nodded. "I want to tell you about a woman I have been counselling for some time."

I blinked, but otherwise remained motionless. He paused long for effect, but it wasn't washing with me and he was forced to carry on. If he wanted me to do a job for him, *he* needed to persuade *me*.

"Three years ago, this woman escaped, and she came to me and told me about a group of twelve. This circle is massively abusive. It is predatory, and at its root, is the worship of darkness."

At that point, he certainly had my attention, but not for the reason he had hoped. I was fascinated by what I considered, to be a fruitcake.

"This woman is now in her mid-forties. She is the product of a French mother, and a English father, from a union made here in Dublin." I began to wonder how she knew where she was conceived, but I let him carry on. "Her mother gave birth to her in France. Her feet were skinned at nine months."

I was looking at this bloke and dismissing him, but that statement nudged me sideways. "This was the beginning of control over the child. She was then returned to Dublin."

He went on to describe the address, an attempt, I imagined, to give the story credibility. Such details were lost on me; I was too busy observing his madness.

"She was the middle child of thirteen. She had an IQ of 168, and could speak eight languages at the age of three."

Now, at that stage, I would normally have got up and left. How could anyone be expected to believe that sort of nonsense? Then I began to wonder why I was still sitting there. If I'm honest, it may have been because the man had significantly unsettled me. He had done so by appearing rational. He made me uncomfortable through his soothing delivery, and his menacing eyes. He spooked me because, for some reason, I could not instantly dismiss what he was saying, and I couldn't understand why.

"She was forced to live under the stairs. The French woman's husband fathered the other twelve children, but this one, "the Heir," had to become the queen, and to be the queen she had to be the middle child of thirteen."

He began one of his pauses, and as he stared at me, I suspect he knew he had scored a point. I stared back, but with less conviction. His thumb rested against his cheekbone, his finger at his temple. "This group is obsessed with numbers. The girl conceived many children between the age of eleven and eighteen, and each time the child was taken to a particular religious order."

He named a nun who he claimed had dealt with the children, but I wasn't taking the smaller details in. "Each child was sacrificed."

He stopped. I stared. He resumed. "She was systematically abused and ignored, indoctrinated and conditioned. Her lacerations were repaired by superglue."

His fingers fluttered then, and as a reformed smoker might habitually tap a pen, he almost stroked his opposite cheek. It was an involuntary gesture, and one which I doubt he was even aware of. The nonsense resumed. "She cut herself and smeared her face with blood in an attempt to become a person, to be recognised. As a punishment, she was hung on hooks in the cupboard and coats were used to cover her face. She was brutalised and raped by the people in the group."

He went on to talk about various people he claimed to have been involved, including a Protestant minister in Dublin, a priest and policemen, and some folk from England. I switched off the story for a while, and zoned it out to a drone, thinking about my wasted journey and his bonkers outlook on life, before eventually coming back to it. "She grew up being programmed and drugged, to be mentored as the queen," he was saying.

I began to question how this group treated their queen. I tried to joke with myself that their command structure needed work. Yet somehow the humour wouldn't come.

"She would then be sent to kill the children of other heirs."

I wondered whether perhaps there really was a woman, and that he had indeed spoken to her, and believed her. He certainly appeared to believe what he was saying to me. "At times like solstice she would be taken away. That's when she was abused, mutilated and forced to do unspeakable things."

My concentration lapsed again, what sort of mind had conjured up this dreadful fantasy?

"I didn't believe her at first," said the Counsellor, "just as you don't believe me now." He started staring again. I had rallied somewhat, and managed to match him. "But you will believe me."

I found myself concentrating upon the man telling the tale, as opposed to what he was saying. I was vaguely aware of some outlandish claims about how the group controlled the woman, and what they had made her do, but I'd had enough.

"What do you need me for?" I felt a sudden need for clarity on what this was all about.

"To keep her safe of course," he said, as if that was obvious.

"Charlie is not a bodyguard service," I said.

"No," he said. "But you could help root out this circle."

If such people existed, I thought I could take a certain amount of pride in rooting them out.

He continued, "I've been walking down streets with this woman when thugs came towards us, and tried to take her away from me. So long as there is a semblance of good, there is no chance that harm can come to her. I and six others stayed with her over Beltane to protect her."

I had no idea what he was talking about at that stage, so I stopped listening. I gazed at his jeans, and his sandals. I looked at his counselling couch, at his shelves, at his smug face, and I got up and left. I drove straight to my parents' house, collected Isla, took her to the boat, and cuddled her to sleep. I didn't let her go until morning.

Eighteen

Jerusalem

I thought about it non-stop. How I would approach her when I saw her again? What would I say, what would I do? I thought about it more than I thought about anything else. I must have, because for an entire fortnight I ignored any sensible notion that entered my head. I rehearsed it, refined it, adopted different scenarios. I built conversations designed to provoke the correct opportunity. In the end, I made a proper bollocks of it.

Of course, the first problem was finding her again. It crossed my mind that she could so easily have stroked me. She had perfect deniability; if I got caught killing the paedophile, no story I could plausibly tell could possibly make her complicit. I wasn't supposed to be in Jerusalem, I had to deny having been in Gaza. As far as anyone anywhere was concerned, she and I had never met.

In any event, the name of the charity was all I needed. On Abu Taleb, not far from the dusty court gates, I found a clunky little café which sold internet time for a few shekels. I looked up the humanitarian outfit, wrote down the landline number for its office in Gaza, and then called it from a pay phone with a stinking handset. The greeting was male, and in Arabic. "Is Shannon there please?"

The line rattled like a drum as the receiver was dropped. I could hear sandals slap off down a hall. "Hello?" she said, eventually. The gentle rise of her voice in query sent a shudder through me, and my planned words warped as I reverted, introverted, to type.

"It's done," I said.

She didn't miss a beat, no matter how disturbing the message must have been. I could feel her thinking, but there was no pause, no panic.

"Are you ok?" That took me aback. She sounded so gentle.

"Yes."

"Is there anything I can do to help?"

As the years rolled past, her endless concern for others would never cease to amaze me, but in that moment, I loved her, and I needed her.

"You could... you...." I paused. Then I threw my risk at the wall and said it. "Would you like to come and see me, before I have to go?"

"Yes."

"Thank fuck for that," I blurted, and she giggled; a cheeky, involuntary, roguish little laugh.

Then there was silence. And it was a beautiful silence. I closed my eyes. I could hear her breathing, and it was calm, and I was calm, and our silence was in sync. There was no awkwardness, just a relief, and an incredible peace, born of incredible violence.

*****

"Tell me about it," she said.

"No."

She paused. "Yes. I want to know."

I looked at her, lying, cradled in the crook of my arm, her incredible eyes upturned to me. "Why?"

I hadn't expected to be asked to recount the detail. "Because it's on me," she said. She wasn't revelling in the man's demise, she was taking responsibility for it.

"It was rough." I had no intention of telling her everything. Back then I was relatively good at boxing up the bad stuff, and stacking it away. I didn't want to go over it again myself, never mind making her go through it too.

"I insist, Sam."

She used my name. Nobody ever used my name. In the Corps, in the Service, I was always just "Irish," or "Ireland," which suited me fine. Shannon always took a different tack. I lay still for a long time, but she sensed she didn't have to press any further. She knew the story would come, and I knew that somehow, every story would come. It was the start of her easing my conscience, becoming my counsellor, my cure.

"I found him easily enough, and I tailed him a little and got to know his ways. I saw what you saw, his desire for kids."

She shifted uneasily, so I paused. Then she ran her hand over my bare chest and squeezed gently; go on.

"I did it at his flat. That night. The night I caught him with the kid. He was with a young fella." I didn't elaborate on what had happened on the heath. "His place had a low veranda, like a balcony, except smaller. I went back to my hotel and waited till the city was silent. I pinched a ruler from reception on the way back out, and when I got there I swung up onto his patio thing, and cracked the door with the plastic ruler."

I paused to look at her, but all I could see was the parting of her hair, the short mane now straggled by exertion. Her hand betrayed her where her eyes could not. Her fingers gently crabbed my skin as the detail was delivered.

"He fought hard. He was lying down when I entered his room, but he was awake, no covers, no clothes. Makes it hard. To get a grip."

It can actually be tougher to deal with someone prostate than upright, and the paedo had been as slippery as a mackerel. "He rolled away as I reached for him, and used his feet. His legs were surprisingly strong, and it took a while to grapple him."

I hadn't wanted his blood on me. I didn't trust his blood, his likely infection.

"I took his foot and used my weight to turn it, snapped his ankle and then had to get to his head because of the screaming and the pain. He writhed and fought and shouted and I had to get it done, but he was strong enough and it took a few blows to pacify him long enough to get to his neck. Then it was over and he was dead, covered from head to toe in my DNA."

She spoke then, out of concern for me. "Can you be traced?"

"Probably. I had very little time to clean him. He made a serious racket, and I needed to get out of that flat. There was no blood so I washed him with a cloth best I could. I don't know if it was enough."

She lay tense against me. "Can the Israelis trace the DNA? To link it to you?"

"Is my DNA on record you mean?"

"Yeah, can they, like, subpoena it or something, from the Brits?"

"Well, it's on record, in the Navy somewhere. They've got my blood and samples and stuff. Bound to have, I've spent a bit of time in the infirmary."

"No shit," she said, as she traced an unsightly scar across my abdomen.

"But I doubt the British would share that kind of information, and anyway, how would the Israelis know I'd been there?"

"They know," she said. "They know who's been in and out of their country. If they didn't lift you, then they were playing with you. Watching you, or tracking you."

She spoke with conviction. Israel was a small country, with a big army, and a serious dedication to its own protection. I had no reason to doubt her sincerity, but it did rather make me question my ability to act covertly. I let it slide. To argue would have been petulant, and pompous; she was probably correct. Anyway, she was lying naked beside me and I'd opened up further than I had ever done, and it didn't feel at all uncomfortable. I sensed she felt she had gone far enough, and she closed it down.

"He's gone now, and kids are safer. That's all that matters."

We never spoke of it again. She never knew about the terrible bludgeoning it took to kill the man, the horrific, skull-crushing blows I'd had to deliver to extinguish him. The way he'd suffered, and lashed around in agony. Yes, the world was a tiny bit safer for some kids, but only a few. I filed it away, and pulled Shannon tighter against me.

*****

If getting into Israel had been hard, getting out of the place was nearly bloody impossible. My inclination was, as ever, to go coastal. I'd only been in Jerusalem a wet weekend, but I quickly got twitchy at the stale dryness, and my inability to see the sea. Wherever I have lived, I have been able to look upon an ocean, or a lough, or an inlet of some sort, every day. I don't go inland if I can avoid it.

Shannon had borrowed a car. She drove me to Tel Aviv, and gave me enough shekels to allow me to spend a few nights in the most disgusting hostel I have ever seen. It was a needle-infested pit, with blood on the sheet-less bed, so I slept on the beach. As dawn broke I went in search of a boat, in the hope that a skipper might agree to take me to sea. But the doubt that Shannon had placed in my head about my DNA, and the extension of the logic around what capture would mean, made me opt for caution. The Navy would throw me to the wolves if I got picked up by the IDF, or Israeli police.

The creeping daylight brought a dose of reality, that my planned escape was daft. I reasoned that a brutal-looking bloke trying to hitch a lift from fishermen, or offering to crew a sailing boat, would raise considerable suspicion. I decided therefore, to steal a yacht and head in whatever direction the charts on board would take me.

And therein lay the first of my problems. Tel Aviv's main marina was incredibly small. I swam into it to get beyond the security fence with minimal fuss. I quickly realised though, how much of a challenge the theft of a boat would pose. Of the dozens of yachts that I broke into, there were precious few that had charts which mapped an area beyond the immediate vicinity. It made me realise the extent to which Israel was surrounded by hostile countries. There was no point in a sailor buying charts for day cruises – there was nowhere safe for them to travel to. To embark upon anything other than a pretty serious voyage, skippers would inevitably find themselves in Arab, or Muslim terrain.

I found one chart, far less detailed than I would have liked. It had Cyprus on it, and the Israeli coast, so I settled on Larnaca as my destination. It was about one hundred and eighty nautical miles away. Too far for a slow, beamy yacht. And so, I gave up on my second bright idea of the day, and tinkered my thinking into another direction.

In a corner of a car park was a bundle of sailing dinghies, and a few racing boats with more substantial lifting keels. These were attractive to me because they were plainly suffering from under-use. The ropes and sheets were gently greening, but the rigs appeared to be in good shape. There was a shed nearby. Through a crazed window I could see sets of sails. One boat was particularly appealing; I didn't recognise the make, but it had a compass, an open transom, and a retractable bowsprit. It was about 20 feet long, and substantially built. I estimated it was capable of between six and sixteen knots, which, with a favourable breeze, could get me to Cyprus in less than twenty-four hours. More importantly, nobody would expect a yoke like that to sail to

Cyprus. No customs officer at the other end would imagine it had come from another country, and so would likely ignore it. If I left at night, it could get me well off shore before anyone knew it was gone.

I used what money I had to buy a breakfast, and to stock up on water, energy bars and sunscreen. I buried my provisions in the sand beneath me on the beach, and settled in for a day's dozing, ahead of the trip.

*****

"You are one lucky bastard." My superior was snarling at me, as he spat out the findings.

"Discontinued in the interests of public justice."

Utter disgust.

I had known that I was looking at dismissal from her majesty's service. On top of that, a hefty fine was likely, plus up to a year in prison. So, I had to agree, I was a lucky bastard. Lieutenant Commanders who appear before military courts don't normally escape lightly, unless charged with some sort of assault. That is almost encouraged. Those up on fraud charges are ushered away into oblivion and never heard of again, in the hope that the press doesn't get wind of what goes on with missing MoD kit. But for absence, and negligence to my team, which was all they could prove with regard to what I had done, I could have been in very, very deep water.

I was due to be listed simply by rank and as belonging to the Royal Navy. I was as amazed as anyone when the charges were kicked out. Only then did it become evident that the nature of Operation Charlie was so sensitive, that my bosses had taken the view that no detail should be given out, even in the comparatively closed environment of a court martial.

That didn't mean I could remain in the Special Boat Service though. My belligerent refusal to go into any detail about what I had been doing infuriated my Major. Despite not having managed to get me convicted, he ensured that the brass busted me back to the Marine Corps.

He was a petulant man, the Major. He was tough enough, and had apparently been a particularly good rugby player in his youth. He'd certainly retained the build. His attitude however, was straight out of Tory central office, and his education had insisted that his compassion was limited to those within his own tax code. Even though I was an officer, he treated me as a grunt, and his men were expendable and distasteful in equal measure. They were his fodder, and I was their well-trained collie.

Part of me wanted to take the hit on the chin. I may have made questionable decisions, but I'd met the love of my life. Provided I wasn't going to prison, a promising new passage lay ahead of me. But the work that had gone into becoming an elite naval officer had been gargantuan. The physical and mental sacrifice took more than a piece of me, and although I didn't fully appreciate the extent of that toll at the time, I had loved being a member of the Special Forces. We got no thanks for what we did, we could never have successful operations acknowledged, but I knew I was at the very top of my game. I knew that few could ever be asked to do the things I did, and I knew I'd miss that terribly. At the age of 35, I was a Marine once more.

Two months after the case collapsed, I got on with things. Shannon and I married in the garden of my folks' house, by the sea, on a sunny day in May. Her family came north, and mixed easily with my own. There were some tough enough cookies there from my rise through the ranks, and all my pals from home. There were no politics, and gallons of rum, and we danced and sang all night as guitars and banjos were handed around. Everyone took their turn to perform, a proper Irish affair. It makes me choke now to think of that day, at the top of the tide. Given how I earned a quid, I never imagined that Shannon's travels would end before mine.

Nineteen

One month after his visit, I checked on the resting place of the man who had come to our boat to kill me. To go there at night was impossible, as torchlight stood a very good chance of being spotted from the mainland. During the day, anyone with binoculars might watch me bump my dinghy up the stony beach, and track much of my progress across the rabbit hole-ridden surface. There was cover, of sorts, in making it look as though I was exercising my dad's dog, because I refused to take Isla to that particular island anymore.

The deep shuck I'd deposited the man into was reasonably well hidden. It was hollowed into the centre of the island, and covered in overgrowth and briars. I counted on the local wildlife, rats and birds, to assist with the decomposition. When I got to the grave, I was pleased to find that there was absolutely no detectable sign of the corpse. It had sunk well at the time, and even the dog showed little interest in investigating. The body's exposure to humid, moist air would help strip it back quickly, but it would take another month to make life properly difficult for a forensics team.

I scoured the press every day for stories about a missing man, but there was absolutely nothing from any part of Ireland that fitted his description. I found that curious; surely someone, somewhere, would miss a hulk like him? I roasted the man's clothing, and I was confident that once the final rashers of flesh were eventually gnawed back, the corpse and I could not be connected.

That didn't solve my issue though, and it certainly didn't mean that Isla was safe. We had sailed to Scotland after I disposed of the intruder, and spent an edgy fortnight, dropping anchor at various points up the Clyde. No matter how secluded the bay I chose, sleep eluded me. Whoever had sent the man had managed to find me, despite our nomadic and unpredictable existence. My destination was the Gare Lough, not far from the Port of Glasgow.

At Helensburgh, I made a call. The company, 43 Commando, was stationed just a few miles north at Faslane naval base. The Fleet Protection Unit was a crack squad of Marines, deployed to protect the nuclear submarines, which slipped in and out of those beautiful waters like enormous black seals. It sounds stupid to say it, but the knowledge that five hundred Marines were based just a few miles away gave me comfort. Commando friendships are hard to maintain in an ordinary sense. We are often solitary people, content to live without dependence. Yet bonds are forged that cannot be forgotten, even after discharge. I hadn't kept in touch with anyone since I'd left, save for a copy-and-paste exercise in response to the sympathy e-mails that had come my way. All the same, I knew that there would be help, provided my buddy was not on leave.

He responded to my request within hours. At five feet four, we'd nicknamed him Mini Marine, and when he appeared on the pontoon beside our boat, I could barely see him over the top of the dodgers. Mini was a formidable and fearless leader though, and the men in his unit would have done anything he asked of them. I'd often heard his Glaswegian accent barking at his team, and too many times I'd heard him counsel them with astonishing softness, following the loss of their friends. He was a signals expert. There was very little he didn't know about comms. We were seconded together to the SRU, the reconnaissance unit, and he and that job fit like a pair of old jeans.

Alongside him was a more awkward-looking character, with a heavy-duty Peli case. Mini didn't even introduce us, he just ordered the bloke aboard and told him to get started, while he and I took Isla off to a pub for lunch. It was great to catch up, and I filled him in on the work I'd been doing with Charlie. When we got back to the boat, the Peli case was open and the delicate kit was being gently replaced into dedicated foam slots. Mini got straight to the point.

"Well?" he said, "what's the story?"

The awkward man frowned.

"You've obviously got the usual traceable kit on board, and a VHF radio, but I'm assuming from what the boss here tells me about you, that you know to keep all of that switched off most of the time. So, the only signals coming off the boat are navigation, the GPS, the radar. The chart plotter could, conceivably, be followed, but it would take a hell of an operation to reverse a signal onto the boat and off it again. There's no tracker on board. There's no unusual signature. It's like I said." He shrugged towards Mini, who turned to me.

"No matter what you think, you're not a hermit," Mini said.

"I'm not trying to be a hermit," I countered, "I'm just keeping my head down, for obvious reasons," I nodded towards Isla.

"If you literally kept your head down you would have stood a chance. But what you don't appreciate is how much of you is recorded. Images, photos, social media, you're there. All someone, somewhere needs, is a tagged image and you're nailed." He looked at Isla.

"Sorry love," he apologised for swearing. I told her to get on board and play.

"But I avoid cameras," I shook my head.

"You avoid snappers with an SLR," he dismissed me.

"I avoid people with camera phones, I avoid selfie sticks. I'm not even in family photos."

"You're on camera all the time. Whoever it is that's after you – all they need is your service-record mug shot. That matches your image to your name, and you're fucked. They can input that image and they can search, and they can find where you were last recorded."

"I haven't even been on CCTV." I thought of Dublin airport, but tried to persuade myself that it was in a different jurisdiction.

"Yeah, you have, and most of it is stream-able somewhere."

"Not near where we anchor though?"

I really struggled with this. I thought I'd been so careful. Turning off location settings, refusing the laptop access to data roaming, or anything that could ping me or where we were anchored, or headed.

Mini sighed, like he was talking to a dope. "You come ashore occasionally right? For food, or work aye?"

I nodded.

"Where do you launch the dinghy from?"

"Mostly a sailing club," I said, content that it was isolated enough to defend myself.

"Which one?" he asked.

I told him. He lifted a phone from his pocket and stared into its enormous screen. He tapped. "This one?" he turned it to me.

"Yeah," I said.

He turned it back to himself and tapped once. "A weather cam, live streamed." He turned it back to me.

"So?" I doubted whether anyone ever looked at the thing. "That's just to tell members whether the tide is in or out, or what the sea state is like."

"It also tells them who's walking across the boat park, and if someone is recording it, this allows them to take your image."

"Bollocks." I began to realise the extent of what was possible. "So, if they can access an image that is provably mine, from a military database, then they can search around the internet to find where I am?"

"If they've got the right software. Restricted stuff mainly. They can tell where you were recently recorded," he said. "It probably wasn't the bloody sailing club, mate, but it could be, it could be the local post office, or the petrol station. Man, it could be someone's home if they have security cameras linked to their Wi-Fi. Anything can be hacked, pal."

"And it what? It maps my face?"

"It takes a kind of fingerprint of your face, and it keeps it. Then all they need to do is to hunt around the area where you were last pinged. Or, they sit at their computer and they nail your position using one of these," he wiggled his phone at me.

"But, I'm careful with that yoke," I said, "I have the privacy settings nailed down, and…"

"Yeah yeah yeah," he said, "then why do you have it? There's a GPS in there, there's a signal to switch off. When you power down, you tell the system where the thing is. No matter what your settings are, your provider and the phone maker know where you are, or at least where you last were. Don't believe anything else. But better than that, there are people that can turn the bloody thing right back on again. They can listen, they can even watch through your camera. Only when the power source is totally and utterly exhausted, way beyond shut down, are you really on your own."

I stood and stared at him. It took a while to sink in. I was hunting through all I had done, all I had said. All those private moments consoling Isla, the pair of us crying and hugging and promising to look after one another. I got increasingly angry, and then turned to him. "But it would take some doing, wouldn't it?"

"Aye," he said. "This is government-level stuff, or super-hacker. This is special ops capability, or a freelancer with skills like that gappy-bearded bollocks," he nodded at the tall guy.

"This isn't great."

"Whatever you've got into, pal, this is pretty serious shit."

The technical bloke stepped off the boat. He didn't appear to have taken offence at Mini's insult. There was no way the man was a Marine, but he definitely answered to Mini, and that type of language was taken as banter in the Corps. I shook his hand and he wandered off awkwardly, the Peli case bowing him to one side. I deleted the few contacts off my phone, changed the access code, and handed it to Min.

"Could you find a place for this? Preferably on board some ship headed for foreign waters?"

He smiled. "I will. It may or may not be the phone by the way, it could be your ugly visog."

With one hand he took the phone, with the other he grabbed my hand, pulled me to his shoulder, and gave me a bump.

"You take care," he said.

Then he turned heel and peeled off. I didn't even need to thank him.

*****

My hire car and I were nearly flat packed by a Luas tram on the North Quay. Dublin had evidently changed a lot in my absence. I turned onto a street I thought I knew well, only to find the silent menace trundling towards me. It had a bell like a pushbike, hardly a fitting warning I thought, as I reversed at speed and nearly killed a horse pulling a carriage full of tourists. The driver's reaction reminded me that swearing is a national pastime in Ireland. The language isn't designed to be offensive, it's simply common parlance, but it makes sailors, like me, sound dainty. I decided to abandon the car and make the rest of the trip on foot.

I'd spent weeks making sure that that my instincts were worth following, that I hadn't missed a trick. I had to work out who wanted me dead, so that I would not get dead when they tried again. I had a child to mind, and a little heart to heal.

I felt sure that I hadn't been compromised through my work for the charity woman. Before I binned the phone, she engaged me about once a fortnight to do jobs. The process was simple; she sent me an address through the encrypted Viber app, I hired a van, performed a recce, and worked out an extraction plan. Then I messaged her, told her when I'd have the girls extracted, and she looked after flights or ferries to get them home. Thereafter it was simply a matter of delivering the girls, and making sure they were safely removed from the country.

The work itself wasn't well paid, but the spoils were generally pretty good. Occasionally there was a bundle of cash in the apartments, most of which I gave to the girls, some of which I kept. Generally though, even with a wedge of Euros placed in their pockets, I walked away with a handsome sum. I found this easy to justify, given the risks I was taking. I had a child to look after, and although this work wasn't as dangerous as my previous job, it was pretty precarious, and risk had to be rewarded. Besides, it had human value, I was good at it, and because of the extra income, I got to spend more time with Isla than a nine-to-five life would have allowed.

Sometimes there was a confrontation, which I admit, I enjoyed. Gnarly, shaven-headed pimps showed up from time to time. Horrible, selfish, callous bastards that they were. Word was evidently getting around, because at some point they stopped challenging me, and ran as soon as they realised what was happening. I would cause them enough pain to force them to lead me to their vehicles, and their cash. Occasionally I would liberate a weapon, and sling it in the Liffey, or some other deep river or lake. But I was always careful, ridiculously so. Anyone who could have followed me was left on the floor of a flat in bits, bleeding and battered, and without their phone. The cars I used were hired using fake ID, and with credit cards that I'd found in the brothels, which were probably stolen. In the end, I always settled up in cash anyway. I never used the same hire office twice.

Fran was loyal to his friends, and a committed ideologue. I knew he liked a pint, and a yarn, but he didn't know enough to be able to place me anywhere. He didn't know what county I lived in, never mind my address. We'd shared a few beers and a few laughs after successful jobs, but I was reserved, even under the influence. He didn't even know I had a kid, or that I'd had a wife. He knew of the website, and could contact me through it, but other than that he joked that I was a bit of an enigma, and he seemed to enjoy the secrecy of it. Besides, he was a tough character, and would likely fight hard to preserve my discretion, even under pressure.

The trust I'd built up with Fran got to a point where he didn't even tag along all of the time. He knew that some shipping companies would never relent, the Greeks being notable examples. There was no point in trying to unionise a ship skippered by a Greek captain. They were likely to tear up the papers as soon as it left the quay. The only option was to rescue any stricken seafarer, and get the poor sod home. Fran got a bit green around the gills when at sea. So, we came to an arrangement whereby he would organise the means to get me onto a vessel, and if I could extract the correct person from the ship without Fran having to be there, he would pay bigger bucks.

On one occasion, in Limerick, I took a bosun off a boat without the captain even knowing I was on board. That was a nice job, largely because the bosun refused to leave the ship without his papers. I was forced to creep onto the bridge in the middle of the night, and break into the ship's safe. I took nearly ninety grand in cash while I was at it. Then we bailed over the side into a rigid inflatable, and were in Galway by breakfast. I gave the bosun twenty grand, his biggest pay day ever, and told Fran nothing.

None of this helped identify the intruder on our boat though. I poured over each job, every single scumbag I'd done over. I knew it was pointless though. I was convinced that the man who came to kill me wasn't connected to that work. There were too many shipping companies; no single one had been sufficiently stroked to hold such a grudge. Even if one of them had taken out a contract on me, it would have been difficult to pin me down. I was under no illusions – anyone could be found. But thanks to Mini, I knew that locating me would have taken organisational support, and real determination. The half-a-heads I'd been battering around Ireland had no such capability. And, in short, I wasn't doing enough damage to warrant the hiring of a hit man.

There was a real and vested interest attached to tracking me down. A lurking shame or consequence, which I had somehow rubbed up. And so, with virtually no contacts, I went to the one woman I knew who might be able to point me in the right direction. I needed to speak to someone in social services, or, preferably, someone who was once in social services. Someone who would have dealt with darkness, and kept it quiet. Charity was the only woman I could think of who might know such a person. After a rather obscure description of what I wanted and why, she reluctantly put me in touch with someone.

*****

I passed the Guinness brewery, which smelt astonishingly fragrant, suggesting that stout wasn't made there at all. Further towards town I crossed the Halfpenny Bridge, and wandered through into the south side, where the accents became more refined and the streets more leafy. Moving east, I crossed the Dart line and under the flickering reflection of Lansdowne Road stadium, I found the address.

The woman who answered was everything I could have imagined. Old Ireland, right there, staring at me with suspicion. She was small, gaunt, and dressed like a 1950s schoolteacher. Hard, uncomfortable shoes, grey dress, cardigan. No colour, no humour. Charity had warned me that she would appear austere, but assured me that inside a tough exterior beat a heart of gold. Such was the old-style care system in Ireland; no smiles, no hugs, be grateful you're getting the nothing that you're given.

I explained who had sent me, and asked if I might have a chat. She lacquered me with a coat of looking-on. I filled her painting time with blether, trying to persuade her to speak to me. Eventually, she stood aside, apparently persuaded that I was genuine.

I walked in to a doily dreamland, musty, dark, decorated for the blind. The cold was striking, the furniture ancient. There was little sign of any means of entertainment – no TV, no radio, few books. I wondered what on earth this old woman did to amuse herself in her retirement. Prayed, perhaps.

"I need to ask you about something a bit bizarre I'm afraid," I told her. She just stared at me. We both remained standing. "It's about a convent in Dublin. Well, partly. It's about a children's home, an orphanage there."

There was a tiny shift in her eye line as her gaze flickered from mine to the barren mantelpiece behind me. I consolidated, shit or bust. "It's about ritual abuse, possibly connected to the seasons."

She slumped backwards, and my heart sank. This was what I'd hoped would not happen. The old woman somehow managed to grip her armchair as she sank, cushioning a surprisingly heavy blow into the tired springs. She eventually looked up at me, somehow shocked and resigned at the same time.

"You see, I've been told about a terrible thing, and I need to know if it's true, or if it's just a horrible fantasy. It involves a child, well, an adult now, a person described as "the Heir."

"Oh, dear God, forgive us," the woman spoke for the first time as she crossed herself.

I didn't take my eyes off her as I bent my legs to sit on her sofa. I just waited as she stared at the wall. Eventually her head rotated back towards me. "Who told you of this? Why would they tell you of this? What did they want?"

I didn't realise it until much later, but that question betrayed an awful assumption. "Is it true?" I ignored her query, but I already had my answer.

She made an unusual gesture, contorting her fingers a bit like the scout salute, but backwards, and placed the tips against her forehead, masking much of her face. The slack skin on her bony fingers was a little unnerving, and stirred some distant fear from a childhood nursery rhyme. I swiped it aside and sat silently.

"It's true," she said eventually. "And my advice to you, is that you drop this."

*****

I didn't feel foolish. Sure, my instinct had been to dis-regard the crazy Counsellor and his hallucinogenic horror story, but in a way, that put me at ease with myself. There was a certain relief that my view of human life had not darkened to the point of blindly accepting what he'd described. I was trying to reinvent myself as a father and a civilian, and my default position gave me hope that I might see the transition through. Still, I'd sought to disprove the story through an independent source, and it hadn't gone as planned. It was a reminder that in order to get us out of the mess, I would need to be able to think the worst, and to believe it.

Once I prized open the crack in her conscience, the old woman treated our encounter like a confession. The surroundings seemed appropriate; cold, claustrophobic, no eye contact. Enormous tears leaked down her cheeks; the deep crevices like tributaries, irrigating the disturbed earth of a freshly ploughed field. The truth eventually flooded her face with peace, as if those years spent suppressing the horrors had wizened her, and left her incapable of laughter, of life. I left her in her exhaustion, but my mind was racing. There were gaps in her knowledge, but her story did keep driving at one thing.

"You are not safe."

She said it three times, and each time it sent a static-like crawl through me. I didn't care if I wasn't safe, I hadn't been safe since I was twenty-two. Isla however, was another matter.

"You have no possible idea what you've got yourself into." The way she began describing what had happened made me wish I was a decade fresher, and fitter for the inevitable fight.

The old girl had grown up in an orphanage, but from what she described, it was nothing short of a workhouse. The children appeared to have been treated as free labour. From her use of language, I could tell that her view of the world was limited; her references were almost child-like and her experience had been curtailed by dreadful hardship and the constant threat of punishment. She described having come of age in the dormitories, and how she realised that she had no ability to live outside the convent walls. Her skills were washing, cleaning, and reading. She explained that she hadn't even wanted to leave; her life in the echoes of that cold, hard environment, was all she knew.

At some stage, when she was old enough, she'd been given the task of looking after babies. They'd come in quite often, but she didn't specify any regularity. Her job was to feed and wash them, and she was scolded for amusing them in their cots. The first time she encountered a child that had been skinned, she looked with alarm at the nun who had carried the child in. "Bathe the feet, and mind your business," was all she was told.

That's what she did, fighting the infection that set in, asking repeatedly for a doctor who was never summoned. Over the years the process was repeated, as the little unmarked graveyard at the back of the building filled up with tiny corpses.

"You become numb to it." She turned to me, the first time she'd held my gaze in an hour. "You, God forgive me, you just learn to accept that little children are going to die, and you try to take away that pain for them, you try to stroke away their cries and their screams. But your mind is filled with them, and your sleep, and you never recover. All those babies..." she trailed off, and drifted back into her torment.

"Who brought them to the convent?" I asked.

"A man from America," she said. Her pronunciation of the continent made it sound like some exotic, untouchable land.

"How do you know?"

"I heard him speak once, to the Sister. He was giving her money. 'God bless your good work,' he told her. He was a small man. He had hair at the sides and he tried to make it cover the top. He'll be dead now I expect."

"He was old?"

"Much older than you, and that was a long time ago. In the 1970s."

"How did you know he brought the babies?"

She turned to me with a furious look, as if I had doubted her. "Because he had one with him."

"I'm sorry," I said, "I'm just struggling to understand how anyone could do this to babies."

"You understand nothing," she spat, before softening. "You do not realise what you are dealing with here. These people will stop at nothing to keep their secret. They even killed a nun."

"What?" was all I could manage.

"She challenged the Sister, told her that she would go to the Guards. It was after a child was brought in and the infection took it. The Sister said nothing and showed her back to the nun, and the next day she was dead."

"Dead how?"

"Dead in her bed. She wouldn't even have been thirty years old. A woman that age, dying in the bed. Sure, who would ever hear the like of that? She was buried in the graveyard, the marked one. Her family came, a brother and a cousin, but there was n'er a doctor allowed near her. No police. Nothing. She was just dead and that was that."

"How do you know she was killed?"

"Because her face was purple, and her bed was...." she paused, "soiled, terribly soiled. And the smell from her poor throat when we lifted her up." She simply shook her head.

I'm no pathologist, but I bought the old woman's diagnosis.

"It was to be a closed coffin," she continued, "the brother made an almighty fuss, but the nuns would not have it. Then a priest got involved and quietened the brother, and she was laid to rest without any more to-do."

The old woman stared at me.

"That's what they'll do to you, if you don't get a bit of sense for yourself."

"Who? Who are they? What is this group?"

"Well I couldn't tell you that," the woman said, indignant again. "Sure, how would I know? Perhaps you should have asked whoever sent you here to my door to open up all this horrible stuff. I don't know what you were thinking at all."

"It wasn't intentional," I told her. "But I'm in it now."

"Well if you're in it, I suggest you get out of it as soon as you can, for these are dangerous and powerful people and they will do anything to keep their dreadful secrets."

There is something about the elderly, when they issue a warning, which is chilling. Perhaps it's their frailty, the slack skin showing their skeletal future, their proximity to the grave, like a head start towards decomposition. Perhaps it's their experience, the corners they've turned long before you. Either way, that old woman unnerved me in a way that I had never before experienced, and in stark contrast to my reaction to the much younger counsellor, I believed every word she uttered.

*****

Of course, I knew that there were other possibilities. The man who had been sent to kill me could have been anyone. A dissident Irish republican, trying to kindle the dying flame of the IRA perhaps. I had served in the U.K.'s armed forces after all, and any military personnel would be considered a target to them. That didn't seem plausible to me though. Car bombs and opportunistic urban gun tactics were more their bag.

I considered whether it might be a revenge attack for poisoning my wife's killer, but I doubted whether anybody would care enough about that scumbag.

The factory owner was a possibility. He was incapacitated, dreadfully so, but he might still be able to communicate somehow. His problem was that nobody on the planet liked him enough to help him out, and I had heard that his power of attorney had passed to a niece. Therefore, his ability to source and pay for a hit had been removed. He was a loose end I should have dealt with, but still, my gut told me that the intruder hadn't been sent by him.

As soon as that brute of a man stepped onto the deck of our boat, I knew there was something desperate afoot. Nobody chooses to kill at sea, unless they have to. There are too many variables – how to get aboard, or ashore, how to dispose of a body, where to leave a dinghy or how to approach without being spotted. Admittedly, that part of the whole assassination attempt still baffled me, but the facts seemed pretty clear. Someone had a serious issue with me. Someone wanted me dead, and they didn't care that I had a child on board when they came to do it.

And so, I think I knew that very night that the reason I'd been lined up for disposal was deep and dark. It wasn't about prostitutes, politics, or seafarers; it wasn't about revenge either. It was about that bloody counsellor.

It didn't take long to work through a likely scenario. As the victim's counsellor, he was probably under surveillance from her abusers. They'd probably pinged me when I met him in Dublin. They may have followed me, in which case they were pretty good. Otherwise I would have seen them. The night I met him I'd had the smartphone with me, an oversight on my part. My eagerness to get the meeting over with may have proved fatal. It seemed more plausible that they had traced the cell phone, or its GPS. That pointed again to reasonable sophistication, and if they had that sort of tech, then they might have been able to discover Charlie. My business had probably told them all they needed to know about my skill-set. If they knew the right people, they'd have been able to hack into databases and find my service records. If they knew where I'd served, and in what unit, they would likely have become concerned. Uneasy enough, perhaps, to decide that I was best removed.

I'd been to countless briefings, and during the surveillance training it was hammered home – the target rarely predicts the lengths to which we go. That was the strength of the U.K. intelligence services, its cunning and guile. It appealed to me, frankly, that those who work hardest and think more than anyone else, get results. If any target were to try to expose the type of intrusion and eavesdropping they'd endured, nobody would believe it. It was too devious for civilians to accept. That's part of the reason I knew that the people who were on to me were professional, well-connected, and dangerous.

I may not have had the evidence, but I knew in my bones that that's how I'd landed in this mess. They'd got to me through the Counsellor, they'd assumed I was working for him. It seemed to follow that such a dreadful group would never leave Isla and I in peace.

Anybody else would have gone to the police, but I knew that they would simply listen to the tale of feet skinning and seasonal abuse rings, and dismiss me as a Nut Case. That's exactly what I had done when I first heard the Counsellor describe the same thing. I could send the plods to the Counsellor, but the police would just take his weirdness as confirmation of their scepticism. He might not agree to see them at all. The old woman would be dismissed as damaged, or institutionalised. In any event, if this ring was as he'd described, it would have the capacity to close down any fledgling investigation. The police had handled my wife's murder appallingly, so I reckoned there was just no point. Even if they did act, it would take too long, and would not keep Isla safe.

It all seemed depressingly clear to me. So long as the members of the ring remained alive, we were in serious danger – me from them, Isla from being orphaned. And so, we had a looming confrontation, rather like many situations I had been in before – take them out, or be taken out. After what I'd learned from the old woman, truth be told, I'd have gone after them even if my life hadn't depended on it.

*****

My priority was to make sure that Isla was safe, and that meant I had a massive job to do. I didn't really know where to begin. I sat and tried to calm the sickening fear that had clotted inside me. Sequencing was important. I wouldn't be able to do anything while worrying about my daughter. With her at my side I'd constantly be operating at half power, always conscious of the risk to her. She was doing so well, and I refused to let my mistakes mess her up.

I took an enormous amount of cash from the bilge of the boat, handed it to my dad, and pleaded with him not to ask any questions. They'd seen a lot of life themselves, my folks, and my occupation had taken its silent toll on them; the worry, the fear that every time a military death was reported, it might be mine. They knew where I served, and what unit I was in, and asked fewer and fewer questions as I grew older. Their attention and care turned to Isla, into whom they decanted their love. I'd often wondered at the shift in their devotion. It was beautiful to watch, the mutual pleasure of simply being in the company of the third generation of their existence, while Isla reciprocated with simple contentment. She would reach for them without thinking, placing her tiny hand in theirs, and in so doing, she gave them purpose, and a sense that their lives had rounded, in some sort of natural order.

Dad knew by the way I asked him that this simply had to be done. He frowned when I talked him through the need to pay for the convoluted journey in cash, but he accepted it. The only thing he argued over was whose cash it would be. He wanted to pay, but I refused. Eventually he took the money and booked the ferry, and I knew that when he got to England, he would secure flights and the three of them would spend a few months in the sunshine. I thanked God for Mum and Dad's early retirement and their health, and then I hunted for a thread to pull, in the hope that I might be able to preserve their safety.

I cast back over the old woman's story again, searching for an "in" point. No matter how much I thrashed around, I kept returning to the same conclusion, unappealing as it was.

Twenty

"So, now you do understand what evil is," the counsellor said gently. He'd woken calmly, despite the fact that I had entered his bedroom un-invited, placed my hand over his mouth, and used it to shake his head. I swiped away a flashback to Jerusalem.

Not here, I motioned to him, staring at the nefarious smart speaker sitting beside his bed. I had quickly learned not to trust any bloody device that could pick up voice commands. If the companies which made them weren't recording, someone else probably was. What a gift to those involved in surveillance; nobody need ever place a bug in a home again. We were doing it for them by selling our souls to convenience.

There followed an odd arrangement whereby he sat on the lid of his own toilet, and I perched on the edge of his bath. He was wearing ridiculous boxer shorts with a gaping convenience. The shower was running as an extra audio precaution, and we talked as the steam built up.

"I understood evil before we last met," I said. "This is not evil alone, this is perversion."

He smiled at me, I don't know if he was smug or seedy, but he seemed to be enjoying it. I certainly didn't frighten him, which I rather regretted, so I needed to find a foothold.

"How did you confirm what I told you?" he asked.

"I second sourced it."

"With who?"

I knew I had him on the hook then. He didn't like the notion of others knowing his secret story. I ignored the question, but hoped he'd ask again.

"I'm prepared to take the job," I told him. "How do you want to pay?" I needed him to believe that my interest was primarily commercial, but he still hadn't got past the previous thing.

"Did she tell you about the others?"

The crafty bugger was fishing, but I had the line. I knew that if I ignored that query too, he would start to spill. He had to show that he knew more than my source. Otherwise he stood the chance of becoming irrelevant. He'd opted to guess it was a woman, which seemed interesting, and I made a mental note to reason out why.

"Cash only."

"You'll get your money," he sighed, as his trunks yawned and I stared instead at the steam condensing on his enormous mirror. Something caught my attention then, but I didn't compute that properly at the time. Something visual, unusual.

"When?" I tried to keep returning to the cash. It would conceal my fear for the future and safety of my daughter, and it seemed like a useful distraction.

"When you deliver," he smiled. There was a leeriness to his grin that somehow coupled to the observation made by my subconscious. I began to reassess him.

"What is delivery, to you?" I used a phrase I'd heard some plummy officer once deliver to his poorly-trained troops.

"Well," his hands opened like his jocks, "that's up to you, but we can't have these people abusing anyone else, can we?"

It was then that I saw the condescension in him, the desire to be respected. Such people are often incapable of commanding such regard, so they cling to the tufts of power, as if grabbing at roots when sliding down a cliff. The desperation of a job's-worth. He sat on his bog lid and treated me like a pupil, and I loathed him.

"I need to meet the woman, the victim," I said.

"Oh, I can't let you do that."

He wanted control.

"Why?"

"Trauma. She's deeply unwell. She needs protection. If she even knew I had spoken to someone else about it, a huge amount of the work I've done to help her would be undone."

The vanity in the man became apparent. This was all about him. I flashed back to his designer ripped jeans. Something I had seen since entering his house was niggling at me, but it was time to leave. I needed a lead, so I poked him enough to provoke one. "You don't even know where the abusers are, do you? You claim to protect her, but you can't. You don't know who they are, the people she's afraid of."

I laced my observation with utter contempt, and made to leave. Despite possessing the intelligence to realise what I was doing, his heart ruled his head, and he reacted to the slight before he'd thought it through.

"You'd wouldn't believe the half of it," he blurted, "people in high places."

His aim was to draw me back, but I needed to draw more from his anger before it ran out. I couldn't give him an inch.

"Riddles and nonsense," I slammed the bathroom door for effect.

It opened immediately, and I turned to find that his pecker had finally found its exposure.

"Close to the President," he said, desperate. "Part of the special envoy's team."

And with that, I turned to face him.

Twenty-One

Like most Marines, I detest wasting time. I like to deal with things as they arise. Issues that linger irritate me enormously. I also prefer straight talk to bullshit, and that's perhaps why I disliked the Counsellor so much. He was a bit of an actor, who liked to play with people and was far too dramatic in his delivery. With him it was all suspense and the suggestion of higher power. As far as I was concerned, the group of people I was looking for was little more than a bunch of abusers, who had managed to merge their horrible fantasies into collective action. If I loathed the Counsellor though, I had a feeling I would hate the colleague he put me in touch with.

Flying out of the States is a piece of piss; once you're gone, you're gone and they don't seem to care. Flying into the States, however, can be a tricky business, and the arrival of Donald Trump made it trickier. There is no way to do it without being tracked. Dublin is the best route in, because travellers can clear immigration before they leave Ireland, and Ireland and the U.S.A. are buddies. I had been sent to America on countless occasions on NATO-related deployments. My visa was still valid, so I rolled through. I knew though, that someone, somewhere, was likely watching my progress, probably from a computer screen. I opted for New York, and then a bus trip, in the hope that at least some of my journey would remain unobserved.

The plan was pretty vague, which annoyed me. All the Counsellor had given me was a cell phone number, and the message that I was to go to New England. It seemed like his way of maintaining some mystery around it all, of keeping his hand in the game. He repulsed me so much that I simply took down the contact detail, and left. I couldn't face the prospect of posing questions. That would have given him the pleasure of holding court, and talking in misty-eyed circles.

I was grateful for the cash I'd amassed on previous jobs, as it removed the normal worries about how to fund such a trip. Marines and Special Forces are not well paid; since leaving the service, I was better off than I'd ever been. The only seat I could get at short notice was in business class, so it made for a pleasant flight. I had no phone with me, nothing that would allow me to be followed without significant effort on foot. When I arrived, I jumped on a bus and crossed the river, headed for Manhattan. There I strolled around a bit, jumped on and off the subway, and eventually bought a burner phone to make contact. The text I sent was brief.

"In country. When and where? Charlie."

It took two hours to receive a response.

"Tremont, Boston. Let me know when you're here."

At Grand Central I queued at a ticket booth, and dropped the burner phone into the handbag of a transvestite in front of me. She ordered a one-way to Connecticut, which was well short of Boston, so it suited me fine. I hopped on the bus and slept a while, as confident as I could allow myself to be, that I'd managed to avoid being followed. I always mustered peace of mind from knowing I had done my best. If I did get caught, it would likely be the contact's fault, not mine.

I trundled around beneath the streets on the "T" for a while, and then found digs in Southie, where the bars looked more Irish than those back home. I tried to beat the time difference by sleeping immediately, to leave me alert early morning.

The guesthouse was pretty rough. There was a family next door, presumably in the process of being re-housed from some project. The mother had only one eye, and one of the sons was chasing the dragon in the corridor as I left the next morning. The tin foil rested on his knees and he crouched, wedged, foetal, between the carpet and the wall. He looked up, startled, when I emerged. The way his hand fluttered towards the small of his back made me note that he could be useful later, but for the moment it was recce time, and I battered on.

I eventually got on Dorchester and walked for a few hours towards town. As usual, I was drawn east, to the sea and the harbours. There was a more direct route, but not a better one. It gave me time to think about the contact, for all the good it did me. He seemed to be confident that he would be available whenever I arrived. I wondered what that meant. Was he retired? Did he work in the area, and if so, what sort of hours would make him be accessible all the time?

The shops were all shut, so I had to wait before picking up another phone, but that was grand, as I wanted to walk Tremont and get a feel for the area, and its landmarks. In the Service, we might have called this an "appreciation," working out the ways in and out, the risks and the opportunities. The big disadvantage was that in plodding the streets so early in the morning, I would stand out on CCTV, and could be accosted by a cop. For that reason, I had on a pair of runners, a trackie end and a baseball cap. I popped in some headphones, linked to nothing, and made out like I was exercising.

Tremont was long and pretty by city standards, but coming from the eastern sea side, it was initially disappointing. The City Hall looked boxy for such an old town. The architecture rapidly improved though, and I allowed a little admiration for the speed at which America was built. There was a small church, right bang in the centre of the metropolitan area, then countless banks and chain cafes. I admired the planners' willingness to preserve green areas, and I could see the sky without looking straight up, which was unusual in some U.S. downtown areas. I paused to look in the window of an armed forces career centre, but my attention quickly turned to the park where I imagined the meet would happen. So bloody predictable, I thought, a park bench in the middle of the open. It staggered me that every movie happened the same way. Why on earth would anyone meet in a public place, potentially observed by thousands, when they could do it in an office, or a toilet, or an elevator?

Eventually the cosmopolitan gave way to the ordinary; hotel and cinema land, then residential, and it terminated without glory at what Bostonians would probably call an intersection. Still, it had all I needed, countless ways out, countless ways in, and I had options for exit North and South. There was nothing at the guesthouse I could not do without, and through the recce, I had identified the means by which I could get to the airport quickly, and unobserved. In fact, I looked straight at it, and it made me smile.

*****

I sat by the paddling pool on Boston Common and slapped together the parts of a new burner phone. The battery wasn't particularly well charged, which suggested it had been sitting on the shelf for a long time. Hardly surprising, given that nobody really wanted phones for phone calls anymore – they wanted computers in their pockets.

"In place, what next? Charlie," I tapped, and lapsed into a thousand-yard stare, working logically through the possibilities, and the connection I was trying to make.

I didn't know who the contact was, but it seemed reasonable to assume that he had an interest in stopping the abusers. I didn't believe much of what the Counsellor had said, but I saw no logic to him connecting us unless our goals were similar. By extension, there would be no point in connecting me to someone who was involved in the abuse. I ran over the last conversation, and focused on the American angle, the claim that someone close to the President was involved. "Works for the special envoy," he'd said. I knew that the White House had maintained a Special Envoy to Ireland, or more specifically Northern Ireland, ever since peace broke out. The aim was to secure business and economic prosperity, but also to wade in with the boots when negotiations between the factions got tricky. My broad sense was that it had been a success, but an attaché involved in an abuse ring? I'm sure I appeared sceptical, particularly to the Counsellor's face, but in all honesty, I knew it could be true. Cover-up requires power, and the ability to keep something covered up for a long time requires a special kind of influence.

Behind every public leader is the person with real clout. It had been such in the Marines and in the military, and my interminable attachments to close-protection units had confirmed that politics was no different. The colonels and the cabinet ministers were often just needy extroverts, who possessed the ability to string a sentence together. They also had enough arrogance to wade through any media onslaught; they needed the attention. I had seen at close quarters that there were good reasons why the backroom boys and girls didn't like the limelight. These were people who enjoyed power so much they wanted to hang on to it.

The cyclical nature of politics ensured that failure, for the elected, was guaranteed. When it came, the breed that lingered behind the politician would simply crown another King or Queen, and sand it into shape. Such people could draw their fix, and their finances from power, yet remain un-seen. When I was protecting politicians in London and abroad, I'd been issued intelligence briefings that went with any "Principal." On two occasions, we were told to be more wary of the advisor than the cabinet minister, because un-specified proclivities could pose a risk.

The phone chimed, I'd forgotten to put it on silent. "Come back tomorrow, noon. SMS me then."

The language suggested an American. I deleted the contents of the inbox and sent folders, rubbed the phone hard to get rid of fingerprints, and hurled it angrily into the middle of the pond. I saw no reason to allow anyone to ping me now. On the long walk back, I bought a third phone from a dingy little corner store, and gave it a charge at the guesthouse. The neighbours were fighting, at least the sons were. I got between the sheets and waited.

I woke to silence a few hours later. The jet lag from the time difference had worn off. I lay and listened, hoping I'd been roused by movement in the adjoining room. Ten minutes later its door opened quietly, which suggested that some of its inhabitants were still asleep. I slipped from the bed, and hoped that one of the sons was on the move. I could hear steps on the corridor, too heavy to be the one-eyed woman. I dressed, and followed.

He turned heel into an alley fifty metres from the house, and must have been needy because he didn't venture far up it. From the street, I could hear his preparation, the crinkle of foil, the tell-tale Zippo flip, the strike. I don't know what he was cooking up to suck, but I hoped it was good stuff. I walked off for a while, and by the time I came back he was just as I wanted him, curled over his knees. He couldn't have been more accommodating really. I wouldn't have to hurt anyone today. I lifted the back of his jacket and his belt practically handed me what I had come for, a 9mm Beretta. But there my luck ran out. It was in shit shape; rust in the barrel and the slider was sticky. Worse still, there was nothing in the magazine. I could tell by the weight before I checked. The kid must have used it for show, or for robberies. America was awash with such side arms, skimmed from the military and available in most unfriendly exchange stores. Still, I took it anyway, and went back to the room. There I replaced the plastic wedge I always carried with me on such trips, and kicked it tightly under the door; simple but enormously effective. Key or no key, an intruder's only option would be to break the door down to get in. That and the weapon gave me enough peace of mind to get some more sleep.

*****

I made contact at midday, as directed, and tried to take the reply in good humour. "Go to where the Puritans lie, by Philips."

I had assumed that the contact would want to take a look at me before he stepped forward, so a run-around was to be expected. I began walking, same route, same pace as the day before. I had an idea of where I needed to go. The little church I'd looked at had a graveyard, which pleased me. In any other major city, they'd have paved over it and thrown up a Starbucks, but the Americans had so little history that they hung onto every tale and title. There was a sign, indicating I was on the Freedom Trail, the oldest burial ground apparently, on the outskirts of a Puritan settlement. Lovely, I thought. I waited a while to see if the contact would hit me up, and when he failed to, I wondered whether he was following me at all. I got texting.

"Ok, I'm here." The response was immediate.

"I think not," came back immediately.

I tried to suppress my irritation, and looked again at the first text. "By Philips," it said. I began to dander around the graves. Deacon Robert Gardner, Simon and Mary Rogers, Mary Seymore. Many were hard to make out, they'd been there since the 17th century, eroded by smoke, and later fuel emissions. Isaac Merrion, Piebec Merrion, wife of Isaac, William Hallowell. Three hundred graves, and not one Philips. My patience was wearing. Perhaps I'd missed something the day before? I ran the recce through in my head, as if replaying a tape, and remembered another church, but with no graveyard. I decided to carry on up the road. As I walked, another message buzzed my balls. I lifted out the phone, imagining the contact was watching me do it.

"Go first to Franklin, then Philips."

This told me he was impulsive, changing his mind. I grew to dislike him a little bit more. He'd obviously made a plan, and was unable to stick to it. That, to me, suggested he was excitable, which was frankly not my favourite trait in an adult.

It happened as I passed the Last Hurrah bar. I'd been alert, so I saw it coming, even though I didn't quite believe it. A vagrant, lying by the side of the main street, begging, had picked me out at a hundred yards and was giving me the eyeball. He had a note scrawled on cardboard, no doubt identifying himself as a veteran. Takes one to know one I guess. He leapt up, but he wasn't keen on a greeting.

"Fucking fag!" Anger roared from his eyes. I moved aside and had to pivot as he followed me. He was a fit enough character, and he wasn't for letting go. He appeared determined to shove his face in mine. "Fucking faggot, fucking faggot!" he yelled.

This was attention I could do without, and like the ripples made when a stone hits water, people circled wide, but stared centrally towards the commotion. The rabid scruff wouldn't let up. Every time I moved away from him, his hands grappled me, and he kept screaming and hurling his shoulders towards my upper body. I quickly tired of the intrusion and the attention, and made the poor choice to drop him. I placed my weight on my aft foot and using his moment, bent my forearm to drive through.

As I connected, something of interest registered out of my peripheral vision, but then it was all about withdrawing. I heightened my pace and listened to what was going on behind me. Someone had tried to help him, and I turned a little to catch him lashing out at the Samaritan with his legs. Then there was a patter behind, and I knew he was determined to follow up. This time, I had no choice. I timed it right as he ran towards me. If I had punched him, I would have injured myself and he would simply have got up again. He was spitting now, so when I turned, I caught him just where I wanted, palms up under his eye ridge. His head flew back, his feet rose and he hit the sidewalk with his skull. Even at that he wasn't entirely knocked out, but he'd certainly lost his grunt. One woman stared at me and hustled away.

"So unnecessary," I heard her mutter. She didn't stoop to help the man though, who was bleeding a bit.

I crossed the road and hunted for whatever had caught my attention. Eventually my heart rate rested and I caught sight of it. Straight across the road was another ancient-looking graveyard. It was surrounded by high buildings, apartments perhaps. The beautiful steeple of a clock tower stood to its left, a real Back-to-the-Future type structure. I had to move away, but I could see that the centrepiece of the graveyard was a cenotaph style monument, on which I could clearly make out the word, "Franklin."

I walked two blocks and then coasted back to the area, removed my shell jacket, and took the sunnies off my head. There was a little blood on the pavement but not enough to worry me greatly, so I skipped up the steps through wrought iron gates, into the graveyard. A man in period dress was addressing two Asians and I had to pan between the tour guide and his captivated audience to see the engravings. I caught the largest headstone, "Philips," and made a note to thank the vagrant with a little cash if I passed him again. Without him I would have walked the wrong way and missed it altogether. This sort of mystery and suspense nonsense would normally have made me very contrary, but I was buzzing like a brothel's doorbell. "First Mayor of Boston," read the inscription, on closer inspection. Then the phone rang.

"You could have just called in the first place," I said.

"Well, you certainly know how to make an entrance." The voice was muffled, but was American for sure.

"I think it's time to stop pissing around," I said, in my best Lieutenant Commander voice.

"Come in, pull up a stool. You could probably do with a drink," he said.

"Where?"

"Right beside where you drew blood, my friend," and he hung up. I looked across the street. There was a classy sign, made of bulbs, "The Beantown Pub." I was quite thirsty, and a little tired of bullshit.

*****

I walk into a pub as a woman might a jewellery shop. I looked longingly at Jack and Jim twinkling at me from behind the bar. They're part of the reason I don't do as much drinking as I would like to.

"Diet Coke," I told the barman. He nodded in an odd kind of approval, and got his funnel frothing. He placed it in front of me, and stood for a moment. I hadn't been expecting to pay right away, so I looked from his apron to his face.

"On the house," he said, quietly. "I finish in a half an hour, we can talk down below."

He motioned his head to the lower, darker part of the pub where TVs were showing sports. Well, there you go, I thought. A barman. I need not have bothered my arse doing the recce at all. I watched him for a moment; he was in his late thirties, but lithe, and confident, like he was capable and comfortable.

"So where do you fit in?" I asked him as he sat down. He'd changed his shirt.

"It's a long story," he said.

I rather imagined it would be.

"How do you know our friend in Dublin?" I tried, meaning the Counsellor.

"Survivors' network," he replied. "I met him at a gathering here in Boston. He was in a closed seminar about healing. We shared."

That seemed like a very American phrase. I knew it would only be a matter of time before he began to talk about "closure."

"Shared what?"

"Umm, how should I address you, Sir?" he spoke respectfully, even though he clearly had the upper crust.

"Charlie will do," I said.

"OK," he shrugged.

I didn't want his name, but he wanted to tell me all about himself.

"I'm from money, Charlie. I'm Ivy League, and we have a big old house in the Hamptons, the whole nine yards." He looked at me, my turn to shrug. "My family and I are… not real close anymore." He got up then, and reached over the bar to grab a coffee pot. He poured himself a mug, and sat down again, waiting for me to ask a question.

"You're going to need to keep going, I'm fresh eyes on this."

"Well then, you'll need to be very, very careful, because what I've got to say to you is exceptionally dangerous."

I sighed. "Exceptionally" isn't a word people use without rehearsal. "So people keep telling me," I said.

"I went home unexpectedly one night, to New York, from here in Boston. I was at Harvard." He paused, and stared straight at me. Not a flinch. "I was gonna surprise my folks. I went around back and there were big cars in the space the staff would normally park, which was weird, because visitors usually pull up out front. There were no cars round back. Not even my mom and dad's. I kicked around some and then I went to the dining room, I don't know why."

He pulled a chug on his coffee mug, and then cradled it in his paws. "Our dining room is kind of like a library, Charlie. It's a big old room with a balcony all around, and two doors attached to that, and two stairways down to the dining area."

I nodded.

"The house was quiet, so for some reason I was moving around it kind of quiet too, and when I opened the door to the balcony, nobody in the dining room heard me."

I followed his logic and had an image of the layout in my head, old dark timber, with a ladder on wheels to reach the books.

"Down below, there were some real bad things happening."

He paused, and then he went on to describe a sort of ritualistic ceremony, at the centre of which was a child. There were sheets, and there was blood. I shook my head a little, and held my hand out flat to indicate that I didn't need to hear the horrors. It was all starting to bring back some pretty bad images of my own, of what my wife had told me, and of what the Counsellor had said.

"Just tell me who was with your father," I said.

He looked up in surprise. "Oh, my dad wasn't there. These were friends of my mom."

That shocked me, but in retrospect I don't know why. I knew there had been women involved. I suppose I just hadn't anticipated that a mother could be associated with something like this.

"Did they catch you?" I asked. "Is that why you're estranged?"

"No. They don't know that I know. I just, well, I just left. Quietly. Then I just withdrew. Dropped out of college, stopped taking her calls, and her money. Started tending bar," he gestured at his surroundings. "She thought it was a phase, or I was doing drugs. She hasn't tried real hard to patch things up."

"So, can you identify these people?"

"I can identify one of 'em," he said.

"Your mum?"

"Well, sure. But I knew someone else down there."

"Who?" I could feel my head shaking as I struggled to keep the exasperation out of my voice.

"My tutor. At Harvard. Well, he was back then. That's why I never went back to college. He's in politics now. He worked in the State Department, then he moved to the White House. He's like an advisor. I've seen him on the news, stalking around in the background. He's Irish, and he's over in Ireland a lot."

Irish, to a Bostonian, could simply mean his name was Seamus. As it turned out, when I pressed the Harvard barman, he was a third generation American.

"And you shared this, umm, this experience, with the Dublin man, the Counsellor?" I asked.

"Sure, I told him, in private. It was that type of seminar, all about healing. He'd come right out and described what had happened to some woman in Ireland, and it fitted right in with what I'd seen in my Mom's house. To hear someone else describe that sort of evil, I felt like I wasn't insane, you know?"

I nodded, although he was offering nothing to link the abuse in Dublin, and that in New York. There could be sick bastards all over the place. "Where can I find this tutor, this advisor?"

"New York, mostly. There's an office on Lexington. It's close by some Irish folks who wine and dine big business people, to try to get them to invest over there. It's part of the deal with the peace process."

There was a certain amount of truth to that. American business had been crucial to the re-building and re-branding of Northern Ireland, after decades of political violence. I wanted to leave, but I needed the advisor's name, which he offered.

"What makes you think that the Dublin abuse and what you saw are the same? That there's a connection?" I asked, Columbo style, as I made to leave.

He sort of snorted. "You really don't know anything, do you? It's the solstice, and the shaving, and the skinning.

It all happened exactly the same way. The head, then the feet, on the same night, on different sides of the pond. The old country and the new. This has probably gone on for generations."

I sat still for a moment and thought. Whether the two events were inter-woven or not was almost beside the point, provided he was telling the truth. I didn't know whether to believe the barman. After all, the Counsellor had introduced us, and I had serious misgivings about *his* character. It crossed my mind that there could be other motives at play behind this dreadful story. Perhaps the barman had grown to dislike his tutor for other reasons. Maybe he'd returned home to find the professor shagging his mother. He seemed to sense my scepticism.

"Our friend in Dublin confirmed to me that my old Harvard tutor had been to a particular convent there – many times he said. It's the same Charlie, damn straight."

This was confusing. "How old is he?" I asked, almost certain that this Professor and the American described by the old woman could not be the same.

"In his fifties I guess," said the barman.

Perhaps a relative.

I couldn't think of anything else to ask which I could not verify myself, so I shook the barman's hand. It was strong and sincere, but he leaned forward with a disappointingly dramatic request. "Sir, you stop these people; you wipe them from the face of the earth."

If I did harbour any real doubts as I emerged to the dazzle of the day, they were quickly extinguished. I was wrapped up in my thoughts, and didn't pay enough attention to what was happening around me. Within minutes of walking towards Government buildings the vagrant was back, only this time his stoop was not so low, and his gait was livelier. It was only then that I realised I'd been stroked. He made his way through the strollers and the shoppers, and he moved fast and determined, darting from side to side on the outside of his feet. I caught sight of him with just enough space between us to react, and I had enough experience with such shocks to sprint through my options.

There are two ways to deal with a situation like that. My preference is to meet force head on. That way the issue is dealt with one way or another and is finished with. The other is to turn and run. I didn't think all this through in a conscious way, but instinct told me that the earlier fracas with the vagrant had been a fishing trip, to see if I was armed. The physical confrontation would have confirmed to him that I had the Beretta tucked into the small of my back. Because he knew I was carrying, I knew he was not alone; the fact that he was prepared to confront me, and probably knew that I was former Special Forces, meant that he had backup. Which meant that I had to turn, and run.

I hate running. Always have. Not just running away, which I hate, but actually, physically, running. I do it, sure, but not well and not particularly fast. *By strength and guile* was our motto in the service. At my age I preferred the second bit. The slow start was hindered by a hankering to fight, and by some stout low-sized Americans, warbling around like bowling skittles just short of a strike. I cut down Beacon, and from that point on, was cursed by the sun being directly overhead. I needed it to find east and keep on going. My navigation was on wits, and my eyes hunted as I ran, trying to find some means of cutting back to where I had started, in the hope that those following me would not think to return there.

I saw some vans marked "Suffolk University," and turned into a parking lot, muttering a prayer of thanks because I knew that students would provide what I was looking for. Sure enough, chained to a lamppost were four bicycles. Mercifully, one was secured through the front wheel, another through the back, and both had quick-release nuts. I left the front wheel of one bike chained to the pole, set the frame aside, and then took the free wheel off the bike chained by its rear. It wasn't a perfect match; I would have no front brakes, but I didn't plan on stopping.

I slung on my sunnies, ripped a Red Socks cap off a storefront display as I cycled past, and made for the sea. I was instantly anonymous. They were hunting for a man on foot – bikes wouldn't enter their field of vision. I reckoned I could get to Logan International Airport in about twenty minutes. No law enforcement agency ever expects someone to escape on a pushbike, but they are like low-hanging fruit, ripe and plentiful, and people naturally look at the machine, not its rider. They are, in my estimation, ideal for extraction.

Ideal, if you know where you're going. All I could think of was east, but as my legs pumped I plotted the geography in my head. There was a bridge, which was not ideal. A bike would stick out like a sore thumb on a highway fly-over, and if I got caught, there was only one way to escape. I didn't fancy a dip in the Mystic, which made me think of a Van Morrison song. But the river was shaken from my mind by the sight of two athletic types and the vagrant standing together on a street corner. They looked around urgently. Perhaps it was arrogance, perhaps it was to test them, but I cycled straight by and they didn't even register my passing. The two strangers were dressed like they meant business; rugged trainers, strong canvas trousers which looked casual but had purpose, and windcheater jackets over body armour. I started to wonder just what sort of wasps' nest I had disturbed.

I kept the wheels turning and eventually saw signs for ferries, which seemed to make sense. Logan Wharf was an option, which felt about right for Logan airport, so I ditched the hybrid bike and started to walk, trying to slow my heart rate before I asked for a ticket. As the boat pulled away from the quay, I looked back on the city and dropped the Beretta overboard. I was glad not to have needed it, even as a deterrent. Next thought, New York.

*****

Lexington wasn't much of a peg to hang a hat on. I had no address beyond that single Manhattan avenue, which probably hosted tens of thousands of people every day. I was tired and a bit belligerent, so I threw caution to the breeze and phoned New York's "Northern Ireland office," and asked for the professor by name. The receptionist played ball.

"Oh, he doesn't work from this office Sir," she said, and duly gave me the exact address of his place, which, as the barman had suggested, was on Lexington. I checked into a hotel by the same name and got some sleep, despite the frightening artwork on the walls.

The professor's office was a skip up the street, hidden in a glass affront to compassionate reflection. Beneath it was a Pret a Manger coffee shop, so I started there. After an hour, I realised that it was useless. I could be on someone's doorstep in New York, and never see them. Finding the professor would take more deviousness than that.

Five cups of wishy washy coffee later, I settled on a plan. Perhaps it was the caffeine, perhaps it was irritation at the rigmarole I had managed to get myself strangled in, but I decided on a direct approach. At a Radio Shack, I bought the closest thing I could find to a go-pro camera, a barrel-like device for sports action shots, which would normally be fixed to a helmet. I then had to buy a fancy leather binder and writing pad, in order to conceal it in the spine.

Back to Pret and then to the reception, where I asked for the professor by name. Americans are so polite, and if you are white and show some authority and manners, you can get far in that country. The security man consulted his computer, directed me to the sixteenth, and authorised the elevator. The lifts in the U.S. remind me of being at sea. They hurtle and plummet like a trawler on the waves of a storm. I had to make like I was meant to be there, and so when the doors pinged, I waltzed forward, hoovering in the surroundings and selecting one of three further reception desks. I leaned forward and quietly mentioned the name of the tutor to an elderly woman. She responded in kind, and in a whisper, asked if I had an appointment.

"If you could tell him I have an update from Dublin please?" I said conspiratorially, and she nodded and hobbled off to an office to the left. I had no idea how this was going to go, so I just stood and waited, and pointed my fancy binder at the old woman's back. I allowed myself a certain amount of relief that he was actually in the office, never mind in the country.

The old woman emerged ahead of a bloke who could not have been more academic if he tried. His tweed three-piece even had leather patches on the elbows. A dickie-bow would not have looked out of place around his neck. When his eyes met mine, his face frowned in a mixture of suspicion and alarm.

"Come in please, Mr –?"

"Charlie is fine," I said, realising that all of my caution was evaporating. The receptionist worried me. I had been seen by so many people.

We sat, and he asked how he could help. I positioned the binder nonchalantly on his desk and came right out with it. "Do you know who I am?"

"I have no idea," he said, too vigorously to hold any semblance of truth. He was panicking, he couldn't take his eyes off me, and I realised he thought I was going to finish him then and there.

"I know about Dublin," I paused, "I know about the convent. I know about the Hamptons. I know that you are part of a group that abuses children, that skins them, that locks them up, that kills them. I know what you did."

He made an odd sort of noise, and stretched his mouth open, as if flexing the muscles on his jaw. I noticed a fidget in his fingers. He gradually composed himself. He looked at the wall, then at the desk, then at my binder, and rallied. His eyes widened and retracted, then some switch inside him flicked. I watched an epiphany, like he had always known this moment would come, and he worked through pre-prepared motions and summoned his protocol. I heard a feint chuckle before he raised his gaze from his hands. Then he leaned forward, looked straight into my eyes, and spoke. "You know nothing Sam."

I have never ever felt a shock like it.

*****

I should not have been surprised that they were on to me to that extent. I knew they had placed me under surveillance. They had done that before I'd even taken the job, which was a measure of how good their intel was, and of their paranoia. The irony though, struck hard; if they hadn't sent that goon to our boat to kill me, I would never have become involved. I simply would not have believed the Counsellor, or taken on his job offer. But I was where I was, and not one bit happy about it.

I turned back as I left the office, to catch a glimpse of the tutor flipping open a laptop. I was familiar with the make, a MacBook Air, but with a thin black cover which made it look like almost any other machine. I could see the glow of the apple symbol through it. It gave me a notion, but I carried on past the old receptionist, and into the lift. I was itching to check the small camera to make sure that it had recorded the conversation.

I didn't bother concealing my return to the hotel; I wouldn't be staying. There I got my stuff together, including the operating instructions for the camera, and consulted a concierge map of Manhattan. I left via the kitchen doors, and went down the street to a CXI, currency exchange. I shifted four thousand sterling. The cashier didn't bat an eyelid. Then a yellow cab shuttled me to an Apple Store on 5th Avenue. Thirty minutes later I had bought a MacBook Air, and a black cover, and was getting various pieces of software installed. The whole lot went into a new ruck, with zips and pouches for passports and camera bits. The order of the little Bergen would normally have pleased me, but I didn't have time to think about anything other than my next move.

At H&M I bought a full set of clothes, and bundled my old ones into my original canvas bag. I was worried that there could be residue from the old Beretta I had stolen from the kid in Boston, and if my plan was to work, I could afford no slip-ups or delays at airport security. With fresh Nikes and the subway, I was propelled back to Lexington, where I found a FedEx Print and Ship, and mailed all of my old kit home. In all, I was three thousand dollars lighter, and virtually unrecognisable.

Back on Lexington I took up a position opposite the Pret, and watched the doors. I couldn't be sure the Professor was still in there, so I decided that if the secretary came out first, I would go with her. If he beat her to it, all to the good. Either way, by nightfall I intended to be outside the Professor's house. At 1730 the Avenue was mobbed. A tsunami of commuters drained down into the subway stations, and I began to panic that I would miss them both. I fought through the wave to stand in the arch of the Pret, and waited twenty minutes before the old receptionist emerged from the elevator and joined the current. She was slow, which made it more difficult to keep pace, but by bus and by foot we got there together, to a nicely-kept little street in a Jersey suburb. Her house had geriatric handles screwed on either side of the door, and a ramp, which indicated to me that I would find leverage inside. A few minutes later, a young woman emerged. She was wearing a tunic, plain trousers, and trainers. I pulled on a pair of gloves.

Ten minutes after the receptionist entered her little house, I knocked, and she opened the door. She wasn't so much surprised as alarmed when she recognised me, but to my shame it was about to get much worse. I couldn't apologise for what I was about to do; I needed her to be scared, for a little while at least, and she managed to remain silent as I bundled her back inside. When I got into the kitchen I saw why. In a motorised chair was an older man, her husband I assumed. He was frail and curled, with saliva dropping from his lower lip. Dementia, I concluded, which made what I was about to do harder to justify, but easier to achieve. She would protect him at all costs.

"I need the address of your boss," I told her.

She stared at me. She was a tough enough nut, and on a different day, in a different place, I had no doubt that she would have defied me. But she was a carer, and that meant the well-being of someone she loved depended on her own health and safety. That was my advantage.

"If I don't get the address, this won't end well," I spoke in a low but steady tone, factual, cold, detached. "He'll watch you die, then he'll be left alone here, with you dead on the floor."

My cards were good. I have always been aware of my capacity to appear menacing, but if she saw me out, I would have to cash in and leave. I stared into her eyes, but couldn't read her. Could she see that I had no intention of harming her?

She broke. Lifting a small pad from beside an antiquated telephone, she wrote down an address, and handed it to me.

I drilled into her eyes before I looked at what she had written. "If you talk to the cops, I'll be back. If this address isn't correct, I'll be back. Do you understand?"

She didn't answer, but I could see the debate churning behind her glare. "Am I going to have to come back here?"

She sighed, and then turned to the pad again. She wrote something down, and handed it over. A new address. "This is his place," she said. "Now leave us alone." She moved in front of the old man, as if to shield him.

I walked around her and removed a scissors from a magnetic strip, and snipped the curly phone line. The old woman shivered as I passed, which felt awful and ideal at the same time. I needed her to remain afraid. "Write down the phone number of the home-help," I told her.

"Who?" she asked.

"The woman who left a few minutes ago. She's a nurse of some sort."

"Why?" she asked, alarmed.

"Because tomorrow's the weekend. I'm assuming she doesn't come on weekends because you're here. I'm going to lock you in a room for one day. When I've spoken to the professor, then I will call her to let you out."

I watched proper panic set in then, before she returned to the pad, and wrote a number down, and handed it to me. I looked at it. There was a silence for a full minute as I waited for her to verbalise whatever was alarming her. "He's not there," she blurted. "My boss. He's flying, tonight, from JFK."

The idea of being locked up until I found the Professor was evidently too much. I kept the pressure on in case there was any more to come. "Where's he flying to?"

"Belfast, but through London – I couldn't get a direct flight."

"When did he ask you to book it?"

She was a blubbering mess by that stage and I knew I would get all the information I needed.

"About fifteen minutes after you left his office."

"Did he make any calls?" I strove to make sure that I maximised this rich flow of information.

"He used a hangout. I never make those calls for him. He does it on his computer, with earphones."

I knew she was telling the truth. She was just too long in the tooth to be dealing with such internet hook-ups. "Do you know what this is about?" I probed.

She paused for a moment. "I assume it's something to do with Ireland. You're Irish, he's over there all the time. You could be IRA."

I actually snorted at that. "Get some food and whatever medication he needs," I told her, then walked into the hall.

There was a box room, which seemed cruel, but I felt I had no choice. If I locked them in a room with a window, she could summon help in an instant. I turned back to find her holding a Tupperware tub and a plate heaped with leftovers.

"Who does your boss speak to? Who are his contacts in Ireland?"

"I don't know," she said. The old woman was gathering a bit of composure, and my time was running out in all sorts of ways. "He flies in two hours. You should get out and leave us be," she said.

"One last thing. Where did you book him in. To stay. In Ireland?"

She looked at me, confused. "He stays at the apartment."

"Where?"

"Belfast. They all stay there."

"They all?" I was exasperated.

"Just who are you?" she countered, now as curious as I was.

"Well I'm not IRA. Your boss is into some pretty sick stuff. That's what this is about."

"What sort of stuff?" she asked, but not in a dismissive way.

"Abuse," I said, and intended to leave it at that. To my surprise she nodded.

"You knew?" I must have sounded incredulous.

"You never *know*," she said, "but I'm old, and I know how malicious he can be." She looked lovingly at her husband. "And I'm wise enough to know how well connected he is, for no apparent reason. How a man like that got a job advising government people," she shook her head and tutted, as she stroked her husband's braw head of hair. "I'm in no position to challenge someone like that." She rounded her gaze onto me. "And I've been around long enough to know that if you're going to stop him, then you're not like him, and that means you're not going to hurt me or Hans." She wiped his chin as a mother might an infant.

"Tell me who the others are, those who stay at the apartment?" I pressed.

"I don't know. He deals with all of that directly. I have no contact with any of them."

"So how do you know there are others?"

"Because I make the arrangements. The cleaning. The laundry bill lists five sets of bed sheets. I book the transfers to the airport. Why would one man need a seven-seat vehicle to pick him up?"

I nodded. "I'll let you out just as soon as I can," I said.

"What about the washroom?" she asked, apparently surprised that I still intended to bang her up.

"Get a bucket," I told her, and took the plate and the tub from her and placed it in the box room. She got a bottle of water and ushered the old man inside. She was utterly compliant, no longer out of fear, but out of loathing for her boss. Then she retrieved a bucket from a kitchen cupboard. I didn't want to consider the logistics of its deployment. I felt bad enough as it was. The door was hinged favourably. It took no more than a broom handle, broken to size and levered against the hall wall opposite, and my own small plastic wedge, to incarcerate them.

*****

I missed the professor at JFK, which was irritating. I'd spent too much time with the receptionist, and when I arrived at the airport the plane was fully booked. No amount of cash could get me beyond the reserve list, and it wasn't until ten minutes before the gate closed that a seat became available. I prayed that I could board from the rear, and sit behind the professor. There is nothing more conspicuous than a late arrival to an aircraft, as the passenger tacks up the aisle like a sail-maker's stitch.

I couldn't see him as I took my seat, but it was a big plane. Even if he took a trip to the toilet he would not recognise me, so long as I kept my head down and my hat on. I took out the Mac and the camera and used them to play back the media.

The conversation with the tutor was audible and in frame, but my hopes for it were quickly dashed. My intention had been to send his admission to the *Boston Globe*, but I was the one doing all the talking. Worse still, he'd identified me by name, and no amount of editing would prove him guilty of anything. I was also conscious that the law around secret recording was much more strict in the U.S.A. than the U.K., so I gave it up as a waste of time and put my head down to get some kip. Then an idea began to form, and I returned to the computer. I fumbled about with the editing software to ensure that I duplicated across only the parts of the conversation where I levelled the allegations at him, and his reaction. There would be nothing else on the computer but the exchange; no documents, no media, no photos. Then I erased my voice, and inserted subtitles instead. Once I had erased the parent file, and ensured that the original media had been properly trashed, I relaxed. It had taken half of the seven-hour flight time to perform the task, but I had achieved something, so I slept.

I knew the professor would be headed for Terminal 5 for the domestic flight to Belfast, so I hurried to get there ahead of him. On the Express train, I connected to the Wi-FI, and used WETransfer to send the video file to myself. The progress symbol ticked round interminably, but it completed before I hopped off the carriage, with just enough time to erase the hard drive.

My plan would require proximity, and it made me more jumpy than usual. The tiredness had exacerbated my paranoia, and the fact that the Professor knew my name and whereabouts suggested to me that he might also know about Isla. I could not shake the nagging fear that his people might know where she was, even if I did not. I was, therefore, out of options; his sick group of friends had to be dealt with in its entirety.

I needed to get through to the departures area, which meant another cash transaction at the British Airways desk, another flash of ID, and another risk taken. My main problem was security, though. Heathrow is tight, and I watched the lift for fifteen minutes, willing him to come through. Just as I began to believe I'd missed him, his tweed came into view. He was fumbling with his knapsack, a kind of throwback from the fifties, very academic in appearance and made of beige canvas and brown leather. His distraction allowed me to fall in behind him, have my eyeball scanned, and to be waved into the queue for x-ray at his heel.

We stood silently, edging forward by pace and by pause. He was no more agitated than most travellers, but it gave me the chance to see him prepare and re-prepare for the machine. Out came his little bag of toiletries, toothbrush, aftershave, toothpaste and floss. Then he remembered something in his inside coat pocket, and after much fiddling, he produced an e-cigarette, which he tried to fit into the clear plastic bag. As we neared the check-in, I had to shuffle with insistence behind him, to avoid being funnelled off to another team by a security guard with a retractable tape. The tutor didn't appear to notice. I watched his un-packing like a hawk.

"Please remove any liquids, computers, tablets, Kindles, and place them on separate trays," called the woman with the plastic tubs. She sounded like a town crier.

The tutor wrestled with the buckles on his bag and hauled out the MacBook. It sat alone in a tray, and I made sure mine did exactly the same beside his. Then he set about unfastening his belt and his shoes. I'd had time to think it all through and was better prepared, so I filed around his back and hoisted my arms though the scanner tube, urging it to render me clear. I got out of the machine with a nod from

a Sikh, and tried to suppress my adrenaline as I made for
his computer. His tub came out directly ahead of mine, and
my heart fluttered as I saw how battered his casing looked
compared to my own. But it was take or break, so I lifted
it, and willed my bag to emerge without further scrutiny.
I grabbed it just as the professor came through the arch.
One movement disposed of the tray between our two, and
the laptop was stowed and zipped in before he had time to
compose himself. I sidled off as he hopped around in his
socks and tried to replace his brogues.

The Belfast flight was two hours away, which offered me
another opportunity. I watched him wander off, gazing up at
the various shops and eateries. He paused at Wagamamas,
where there was a queue for tables. Then he moved on. I
followed at a distance, until he turned back, apparently
having changed his mind. I had no choice but to proceed,
and berated myself for having got over-confident. It can be
easier to miss someone at close quarters than at a distance,
and if he copped me now, a lot of work would go to waste.

He eventually returned to join the queue for the Japanese
food, and I could afford to take a break and wash my face.
I bought some sticking plasters at a pharmacy. When the
queue was gone, I was ushered to a spot overlooking the
concourse. The professor was sitting at the bar. We were
two single travellers eating in silence, backs to one another.
I could see him, but only just, in the reflection of the glass
in front of me. I had no idea whether he would do what I
needed, but I couldn't take my eyes off him. The waiter was
happy for me to accept his recommendation, whatever it
was, and I ate without looking at it.

Only when he had finished, did the professor fish around
at his feet and draw out the laptop. If he noticed anything
wrong with it, he didn't show it, and I allowed him time to

flip the top and boot it up. When I heard the start-up chime, I slowly began to make my move. I took the phone, stroked it into video mode, and swivelled my stool to aim the camera at the stainless hood above the tutor. The shot, however, was rubbish, so I had to risk it and get in close. Putting the phone to my ear, I walked over and reached in between the professor and the woman beside him to grab a basket of soy sauce and forks. I loitered longer than was decent. I had no idea whether I had what I needed, but I had to get out.

Back in the toilets I sat on the pan, phone in hand. Turning down the sound, I consulted the video, convinced that my good luck was sure to run out. I watched it all back, my clumsy attempt to catch the reflection above the professor's head, the meandering stretch for the sauce, and then, thanks be to God, in the bottom left hand corner of the screen, was the flutter of his fingers on the keyboard. I caught five letters, VISIT, before the image moved out of shot. I heard him stroke three more keys.

I opened his laptop and stuck a plaster over the webcam, then paused. There are about 80 possibilities on a laptop. I strained to remember the briefings we'd been given on observation training, the old DET instructors revelling in their connivance and cunning. Breaking passwords had been mentioned, but I could not recall anything specific. I sat on the shitter and went for the obvious, simply adding ING to the password box; it vibrated to indicate a mistake. ORS I tried instead.

I was in.

Twenty Two

It turned out that we weren't on the same plane to Belfast, but it didn't matter. I knew exactly where he was going. The drop off address was in the taxi booking confirmation e-mail sent by his secretary, who was wedged in a box room with her demented husband, three-and-a-half-thousand miles away. I would make the call to the nurse in a while, but there was one more play to make before I could release them. I had a feeling she would understand.

The doom set in on home turf.

It was always thus. On tour, I'd been able to focus on the job, on killing and not being killed. It wasn't until I got leave, that the horrors returned.

When I got back to Belfast City Airport, there was no escaping the guilt; the magnitude of the responsibility I had heaped upon my parents, or the uncertainty I had about how safe they were. I knew they would protect Isla with everything they had, but they were civilians, kind, and gentle people. They were also blissfully unaware of what was really going on.

I hired a car at the airport and on the Newtownards Road, I stopped at one of the few phone boxes left in the city. There I dialled my dad, then my mum, and got no answer from either. I ached to hear Isla, and had to work hard to reduce my heart rate and purge the panic. I reminded myself over and over that my folks didn't always answer their phones, and didn't always have them in their pockets. I imagined them having evening dinner at a beach restaurant, their cells buzzing away in a car or a hotel room. But the noise was returning, I could feel its whine. It started somewhere in my inner ear, and although it felt as though it had been there all the time, I only became conscious of it when that bottomless foreboding crept in.

I dialled again and again, each time becoming more agitated. I allowed myself the anger. I knew it would have to surface before it could be purged. Before long there was blood everywhere, and the handset was in pieces and my jeans were torn from what remained of the glass walls of the phone box. The frenzy slowly subsided as I slumped in the cubicle, utterly helpless to protect my daughter, and my parents from a threat I could not be sure they faced.

Such outbursts are not down to PTSD alone. I did experience anger attacks before I became a Marine, and ironically the trouble they got me into became part of the reason I ended up in the military. But the service just channelled the violence, and gave that occasional anger a grip that my teenaged years could not have imagined. Nobody came near the phone box, needless to say. As I calmed, my attention shifted from what I couldn't do, to what I could do, and I got back in the car.

The apartment was on one of Belfast's finest streets. Trees lined the wide avenue, which had pillars at either side of the entrance, one way in, one way out. The car I had rented was easily the least expensive of all on that road; even the children of its inhabitants drove more up-market models. The apartment took up the top of the four-floor building, and the lights were on. There was a balcony, and the professor was home. I knew because he came out after a few hours to puff away on his vape. I worried that there might be someone else inside who might object to his habit, but I saw no evidence of company. If there was nobody else there, it suggested routine.

I looked up at him from the anonymity of my parked car, musing on the fact that less than 18 hours had passed since I had confronted him in New York. I wondered how he would react if he could see me now, sitting below him. The upper hand is important, psychologically. I reckoned he would think I was still in Manhattan, scrabbling around for a lead. His ignorance gave me a certain degree of comfort, but not as much comfort as the realisation that I could see his legs quite clearly. The base of the balcony was made of glass plates. I decided to wait a while longer to establish his routine. An hour later he appeared again in a plume of vapour, gnawing on his pipe, before sliding the door to return inside.

Eventually another light came on, followed by the first light going off, and then a softer glow beneath a blind. The recce had given me plenty of time to think. I knew from the receptionist that there were potentially five bedrooms in the apartment, but there was a light in just one. I felt strongly that he was alone, for the moment, but that it was too soon to deal with him. I needed to interrogate his computer properly. He would be able to locate it as soon as I connected it to the internet. I know my way around tech pretty well, but I decided I needed expert help.

*****

I drove straight to Dublin and appeared, unannounced, at midnight, on the doorstep of the charity woman. She was, of course, enormously impressed, but agreed to help. Her twin was similarly amused to be hauled out of bed at that hour, but by 1 a.m. her face was aglow with the reflection of the tutor's computer. Within minutes there were wires going into and sticking out of it, as she copied the entire contents onto a stick the size of my finger.

"Ah, bollocks," I heard her say, about twenty minutes into the process.

"What is it?" her sister asked.

"He's got an MDM, it's wiping."

I knew broadly what that meant, some sort of mobile device manager. I just closed my eyes and prayed.

The twin worked furiously with the keyboard and then the cables. "Ok, now we see what the diddly-dory is," she said, as she untethered the tutor's computer and stuffed the drive into her own laptop. "Ah it's grand. His hard drive's all there, that's it all cracked too. There shouldn't be any files you can't see."

I was tempted to get her to help me navigate around its contents, but I was more tempted to do something else while it was still dark outside.

"Can you find a number for him, a contact number?" I asked her.

"Sure, it'll be here in his text messages." She stirred two fingers around the track pad.

"Oh, an American number," she said, and read it to me. I wrote it down on the back of his receptionist's notepaper.

"This is all totally illegal like," the twin said, "but if she's involved," she nodded at her sister, "I'm sure it's all for some worthy cause."

For the first time since my wife died, I hugged a woman I wasn't directly related to.

*****

Twenty minutes later, I bought yet another burner phone from an Indian man at a service station, on Dublin's M50. It was a tiny place, cheap as chips, and its security cameras were dummies. Then I roasted up the road at over one hundred miles an hour. At my dad's workshop, I was surprised to find my FedEx'd bag had beaten me back. I threw a wrap of pozidrives, a socket set and a suction handle into it, and headed for Belfast. I gave a lot of thought to the practicalities of my next move, and virtually none to the implications. My mind craved relief.

I thanked God for the affluence of the people on that Belfast street. That type of wealth could purchase privacy through influence on the city's planning committee. The apartment block occupied by the professor had been designed with meticulous attention to detail. No balcony was visible from the windows of any other flat, and the lush trees gave me just about enough cover to clamber up, my tools swinging precariously from my belt.

Four a.m. is dead hour, the period when virtually nothing happens. It is the decent period between asleep and awake. I knew this from countless dreadful hours spent on surveillance – in gutters, in refuse sites, on cliffs and in cars, watching bad people get rest, while my limbs seized. By 4 a.m. I had unfastened the glass floor of the small balcony, and raised it against the balustrade. By 5 a.m., the professor was dead.

Suicide seemed to me to be the best option. Murder would invite vigorous inquiry by the police, but of greater concern was what the professor's friends would make of it all.

It was incredibly easy, really. All I had to do was call him. I debated what to say, but nothing seemed fitting. Nothing that would definitely achieve what I wanted. So I chose just to spook him. I needed him to know I was close by; I needed to place him under pressure, so that he would move without thinking. I also needed him to move in the right direction. The phone rang three times before he answered.

"Hello?" he sounded like he had managed to get to sleep.

"You're in Belfast, you're in an apartment, and you're finished," I said, and ended the call. Then I watched.

No lights came on, which didn't surprise me. I imagined him lying there, stock still, computing. He was not a physical man, he would interrogate the silence and worry that there was someone inside the apartment. He might stay in bed and wait for daylight, which was alarmingly imminent, but he might eventually take a look around. Fifteen minutes passed and I knew that my window to make this clean and easy, was closing. I stared at the balcony doors and ground my teeth.

Suddenly a tiny blue dot appeared behind the glass, which confused me initially, until it partly illuminated a small fog, and I realised it was his vape working furiously. He was looking out. I hunched over in the seat and held the burner phone between my knees, found settings, and removed the caller identification. Then I texted him.

"You have been compromised. He's coming to the apartment. Find a back way out." Which did the trick.

I sat up and saw the glow of his phone as it received the message. Then I caught a glimpse of his face as the French door slid back, and then nothing.

It was silent. I didn't even hear the impact. Fumbling for the car's internal light switch, I made sure it would not come on when I opened the door, and walked over to where the professor lay. He was totally and utterly dead. His shoulders had somehow hit the ground first, his head stove in to his chest. I found his phone in his dressing gown pocket. Incredibly, it was largely intact, save for a crack across the screen. I used his cold dead thumb to unlock it, and then took it around behind a set of bins to re-set the pass-key. The last attention I paid to it was to place it in airplane mode, and then I dropped it into my own pocket.

The climb to the balcony was easier because of the adrenaline. The risk was higher given that I was now a killer; previously, I'd been just a burglar. The glass was replaced with greater care than it had been removed. The post-mortem examination would show no evidence of bruising or pushing, there were no fingerprints, and it would be assumed the Professor had jumped. I was gone by 5 a.m.

It was enormously satisfying, and it was the biggest mistake I could have made.

*****

The burner phone went into the Lagan River as I crossed Shaw's bridge, closely followed by the professor's laptop. I was freezing, because I was tired, and I needed either coffee or sleep. I wanted to get to the boat, fire up the Eberspacher heater, and interrogate the tutor's files.

Once aboard, I realised how big my error had been. It took an hour to erase my laptop, and replace it, in its entirety, with his. I couldn't do it all without connecting to the internet, which was a huge risk, but I realised I had no choice. Eventually, I tapped my way through his folders and became increasingly frustrated at the lack of detail in there. Much of it was work-related – strategy for investment, advice for media communications, copies of speeches. His e-mail seemed very regimented, very factual and perfunctory.

There was an application on the desktop I was unfamiliar with, which appeared to be a video-conferencing tool. I hammered around it for a while looking for a record of conversations, but it looked like a live streaming hook-up app, probably a bit like Skype. However, there was another application which appeared to have the means to capture and record whatever was shown on the screen. That seemed like an exciting prospect, but I struggled to find any evidence that the professor had made any such recordings. I went back to the hook-up software, opened his profile, and found the last number dialled. It was scribbled down on the increasingly dilapidated piece of paper the receptionist had given me. Then I became distracted by guilt; the old woman and her husband were still locked up, and my conscience forced me ashore to make the call.

If the professor's friends were tracking his phone, I wanted to confuse them as much as possible. I drove fifteen miles before stopping, and pulled out the handset. What harm, I reckoned. Using it would only serve to blow more smoke around the place. If some copper did manage to piece the crazy pattern together in years to come, I deserved to get caught.

Ten a.m. in Belfast was 5 a.m. in New York. I dialled the number the receptionist had given me.

"Yes?" the nurse sounded alarmed.

I put on the best North American accent I could manage. "I'm calling about the old lady, and," I paused, realising that I didn't know her name, "and her husband, umm, Hans."

"Hans is her brother," came the curt reply, which taught me not to make assumptions. "It's the middle of the night. Who are you, what's going on?"

"They're stuck, in a room inside the house. I don't have time to go into detail, but they need help. Can you help them?"

"Sure, of course, are they ok?"

"They're fine," I imagined, "can you go now?"

"Uh huh, I'm getting up right now."

"Thank you so much," I said, and tapped the big red button.

The receptionist and Hans had been banged up for a full day and a half. I had caused them pain, but I could live with it. It was time to move on.

I was about to swipe the phone back into airplane mode, when something occurred to me. Someone involved in the professor's brand of grotesque behaviour might want to maintain some form of insurance policy. He was part of a group after all, and groups often argue, individuals fall out. If one of them was compromised, what was to stop that person from betraying the others in return for some sort of leniency?

I stared at the phone and put myself in the professor's place. He was, by definition, a clever man. If he'd made any sensitive or secret recordings, it would make sense that he would not keep them on his hard drive. Computers are cumbersome. You can't take them everywhere with you. They break, and he had learned the hard way that they can get mixed up at airports. So, if not on a computer, where would he keep an insurance policy? On a pen drive or an SD card? Probably, I thought. But drives and cards can be lost or stolen more easily than computers, and in any case, one requires a computer to view the contents.

I had no reason to get excited. It was a very long shot, but the phone in my hand seemed to offer an opening. Staring at the settings option, I began to wonder whether he might keep his insurance on hand, or actually *in* his hand.

I punched in the new code I had assigned to the professor's phone, and swiped through to his photos folder. It was empty. My heart sank a little. Then I opened his iMovie, which was also empty. I thumped my head back against the headrest, and allowed the frustration to pass. Realising that I had left the phone live, I went back to trigger the airplane mode once more. In settings and in haste I nudged the screen, and the option for iCloud caught my eye.

While I understood the premise of cloud technology, I wasn't a regular user. I knew that everything was stored on a server somewhere. It saved space on devices, until the user dragged down whatever music or movies they desired. I messed about in the options for a while, but it didn't seem obvious to me how to view the contents of his cloud. I realised however, that if he did have any photos or videos, I might be able to share them with someone else. Assuming he kept them on the cloud at all.

But who to share them with?

I could only remember a few e-mail addresses by heart; my parents and my dead wife's. And, of course, Fran, and the charity woman. I had no desire to involve anybody new, so I appealed to Charity. "Hi," I said, when she picked up.

"Do you never sleep?" she began.

"I need another favour," I said, "is your sister there?"

"She is."

"I want to share some photos with you, but I can't see them. Maybe she can talk me through it? I'm sorry, it's complicated. I don't even know if they're there."

"I have no idea what you are talking about, so here, talk to her."

The phone rumbled as it was handed over, and I could hear a few mumbled words of explanation. Then the twin came on the line. There followed a list of instructions and actions I will never be able to re-trace, but after five minutes I was put back onto Charity.

"So, I think I've shared an iCloud account with you. Can you have a look and see if there are any videos or photos on it, please. I'll call you back shortly?"

"I'm tied up all morning. Will this afternoon do?" she asked.

"No, I'm sorry, it's really important. Can you have a look, please?"

"Right, so, I'll call you back as soon as I can. And Sam?"

"Yes?"

"I'm really grateful for all you've done, but this is wearing a bit thin now."

"Understood," I told her. "But again, this is really important."

"Is it dangerous?" she asked. I hadn't the heart to lie to her.

"For me, yes. For you, I don't think so, but honestly, I don't know yet."

Twenty-Three

I drove to the closest town and fed coins into a public phone, like rounds into a gun belt. My forehead rested against the glass, my eyes closed, as ring after ring became a dead tone. At least I knew my folks' phones were charged, which suggested they were ok. But then if everything was grand, why would they not answer? The sickness in my gut grew and grew, and I debated whether to buy another cell phone and text them the number to get in touch. But in my tiredness and twisted logic, I feared that someone else might be keeping their phones alive, in the hope that I would do just that. That would allow such a person to trace my movements, and leave me unable to do anything.

I had no clear idea of where Isla and my parents were, and racked through the scenarios involved in finding out. The next call I made was to a Naval base in Scotland. "Min, it's Sam."

"How are you getting on, pal?"

"Not great, Min. I need another favour. If you trace some mobile phones, old ones – not iPhones – can other people see that trace being activated?"

"The short answer is, I don't know mate, but I can find out."

"How long will it take?"

"Well, the long fella you met at the marina, he's the boffin. He's on exercise, but I could get in touch. Are you in big diffs?"

"Isla could be."

"Right," was all he said, understated as usual, but he got it.

"If nobody else can track the trace, can you do it for me? The phones belong to my parents. They're minding her, and they're AWOL."

"Shit. It'll be at least twelve hours before I can do anything pal."

"Thanks Min," I said, and hung up.

Then my service rituals began to surface. When you can realistically achieve nothing, rest, or eat. The time will come when you need energy. I went back to the boat, rolled onto my bunk, and closed my eyes.

*****

Three hours later I woke in a panic, I hadn't intended to sleep for more than one hour. I didn't want anyone to know where the boat was moored, and I was, by that stage, utterly paranoid about using cell phones. So, I used the boat's VHF radio to make a ship-to-shore call, routed through the Isle of Man.

"Where have you been?" The last thing she sounded was charitable. I ignored the question.

"Is there anything on the cloud?"

"Yes, and it's fucking frightening. For you. And now, I think, for me."

*****

The ship-to-shore call had turned fractious; the charity woman had steadfastly refused to e-mail or transfer any of what she had found, and I'd heard her sister in the background, instructing her not to say anything further on the line. She told me to meet her at the usual place, so I hit the road and parked outside the Applegreen Garage on the M1, just north of Dublin.

Ninety minutes later I watched as Charity hurried over to my rental from her hairdresser's car. Her twin was behind her, and she climbed into the back seat. Both looked angry. "What the actual fuck have you got us in to?" the sister barked at the back of my head.

"What's on the cloud?" I turned to the charity sister, who looked more terrified than cross.

"Show him," the twin said, "I don't fucking believe this," she muttered.

The charitable sister pulled an iPad mini from her bag. "We've watched three recordings so far."

The twin chimed in. "They're encrypted. I have special software. It takes ages to process them. It's churning away in the background."

"How many are there?" I asked.

The screen lit up then. "That's another one cracked," said the twin. "Play it, Sis."

Charity shook her head. "No, he needs to see them in order. Otherwise we'll all be as confused as each other. Here's the first one."

She tapped the screen and two boxes appeared, one larger than the other. The heads and shoulders of two people appeared, apparently looking towards their own web cams. On the right was the Professor, but the main talker was a man with a refined English accent. He was well-tended, not a hair out of place, a club tie round his neck, and a golf tan. He was doing the talking. "How can we be sure this man, this stranger, knows anything about us?"

The professor replied, "the Keeper said he seemed to know a lot."

"And how does the Keeper know this?"

"The Keeper is well-connected," said the professor.

"Well, what does the Keeper intend to do about it?" said the Brit, as if he were herding snakes.

"He'll move the Heir," the Professor paused, "in case any of us are compromised."

The Brit grunted. "I'll get the Stranger looked into. We may be best to nip this in the bud."

"Agreed," said the Professor.

"And he's Irish, this chap?"

"Apparently," said the Professor.

"I may need you to go over there," said the Brit.

"Whatever you need," was the reply, and the recording ended.

I had a horrible feeling that I might be the Stranger. I also had questions. "So who is the Keeper?"

"Who are any of them?" asked the sister.

"I know the one in the tweed," I said. "He's an American university professor who was involved in an abuse ring. I don't know the posh Brit."

"We don't know who the Keeper is," said the twin. "But you need to keep watching." Charity tapped another file.

There were three squares this time. The Brit, the Professor, and a younger man. He was skinny, in a t-shirt, and in his forties. The Brit was running the show.

"This is our investigator," he introduced the new man to the Professor. "He's been looking into the stranger. I believe the news is not good."

"Oh?" said the Professor.

It was the new man's turn to talk. He sounded French. "The Stranger is a dangerous man. He is kind of a bounty hunter, and was Special Forces officer for some years."

It was uncomfortable to hear the background I'd tried so hard to conceal discussed openly in front of others. The Brit broke in. "Ireland has Special Forces?"

"He is SBS, Special Boat Service, and Royal Marine Commando."

"Oh dear," said the Brit, in a rather understated fashion.

"Like a U.S. Navy Seal?" said the Professor.

"Rather worse, if such a thing were possible," mumbled the Brit. His eyes were closed, but his face still managed to convey resignation.

"He is resigned. Not long ago, actually," offered the Belgian.

I wondered where this twerp was getting his information.

"So how much does he know and where can we find him?" asked the Brit.

The Professor took the first part of the question. "The Keeper's information is that he knows enough, but, uh, perhaps that's for a discussion off-line." He appeared coy in front of the investigator. That suggested to me that the investigator was hired in, rather than a member of the abuse ring.

"He lives on a boat," said the new man.

My heart sank.

"Of course he does," said the Brit, exasperated. "Where does he keep the boat?"

"Nowhere. He moves around. He sails from place to place. Mostly he's in Northern Ireland. Sometimes he just – vanishes," said the Belgian, with a flourish.

"What does he want anyway? Who is he working for?"

The Professor broke in, keen to show that he had information. "He's working for a group that helps trafficked women. Some sort of charity."

Charity paused the recording and looked at me. "I can't understand this bit. This has nothing to do with us, does it? I never asked you to look at an abuse ring. What have these people got to do with my organisation?"

I looked back at her. "I genuinely haven't a clue," I said, "keep it running, maybe it'll become clear." She tapped the arrow.

"The Keeper described him as a kind of mercenary, a freelancer if you will, rescuing women from pimps," said the Professor. "But the Keeper didn't know anything about his background."

"I still don't follow how that fits our picture," said the Brit. "But we can't have him vanishing." He appeared to address the investigator. "We will need to know where he is. At all times."

"Is possible. Lemme see what we can do."

"That's all for you, for now."

The investigator's image left the screen. The Brit and the Professor kept talking. The Brit looked deeply concerned. "Could the Heir have contacted a charity?"

"I don't know," said the Professor, "I doubt it."

The hairs stood up on the back of my neck. This seemed to confirm the Counsellor's story, that the Heir had come to him for help. I looked at the Brit, and imagined that I was staring at the leader of the abuse ring.

The professor turned even more sheepish. "The Keeper suspects we have a breach."

"There has never, ever, been a breach," said the Brit.

"I know," said the Professor. "A breach would be unthinkable."

*****

It was bizarre, listening to these people piecing together a picture which I had been trying to build for weeks. I wanted to watch the other videos, but Charity needed clarity.

"So they think *I* engaged *you,* to help this "Heir" person?"

"Who is the Heir?" screamed the twin, from the back.

I exhaled, then reeled back in the hope that the three stories would somehow become one. "About a month ago, I got a request for work, through the website you set up for me."

"Yeah," said the twin. "I know, I checked."

I let that pass without comment. "So, I went to see the bloke who had this job. He told me this cock-and-bull story about a woman who was being abused. It was grim stuff, and involved the seasons and all sorts of crazy stuff. He called her "the Heir.""

I looked to Charity for a reaction, but got none. "I assumed you had referred this bloke to me."

She shook her head. "Other than Fran, I only ever sent one fella to you, a counsellor from Dublin."

"A psychologist?"

"Maybe. He told me he was a counsellor. He was sort of – elusive or something."

I looked back at the road. "Well, that's when it all started. I didn't believe the Counsellor bloke at all. But then someone came to the boat one night. I don't know how he got aboard, but anyway he came to kill me…"

"Sweet and gentle…" the sister began in the back, but I cut across her.

"And after that I came to you looking for someone who might explain what was going on. And you put me in touch with the old woman from the convent."

"Who's now dead," said Charity.

"What?" I said.

"Yeah. She got killed during a burglary. What had she got to do with anything?"

"It's complicated," I said, my mind racing. "She knew about a cover-up of an abuse ring. It seems to me now that it's the same ring that the Professor and the Brit seem to run."

"Right," said the twin. "So they're killers. They think my sister tipped you off about some "Heir" person, and now they've got a failsafe way to get to you."

"What?" I turned to face her. "What way to get to me?"

"Well Sam," said Charity, "apparently, *you* have a daughter."

*****

Alarm is mental, yes, but it can also be physical. Fear had never made me sick before, never. But I threw open the car door and vomited hard, my darkest fear realised. There are times when deep tiredness and panic can mix to help you focus concentration on one thing, and block out all else.

The third recording drew my mind in so tight, that I managed to finally zone out the fractious twin on the back seat, and work through what was happening. I listened intently. Every word spoken took on a fresh importance.

The investigator recounted my recent movements. He told them that I'd flown from Dublin to New York. He said that I appeared to be following some undefined lead, and that he'd been cracking my phones from time to time, but that I was discarding them. He said I was headed northeast, and then the Professor chipped in. "I know where he's going," he said, "he's going to Boston."

The Professor obviously didn't want to elaborate on how he'd been compromised by one of his students, in a Long Island library. "I can get our people to deal with him there," he said with confidence.

"We thought that when we sent someone to his boat didn't we?" said the Brit.

"Well," said the Professor, "we still don't know for sure what happened there. The man we sent didn't actually…"

"I know!" yelled the Brit. "He bloody vanished, like this bloody Commando keeps disappearing."

Charity looked at me. I shook my head. It wasn't the time to get into more explanations.

"Well," offered the investigator, "you could wait for him to collect his daughter."

I tried not to pant, but my chest heaved at the mention of Isla.

The Brit placed his face in his hands, and exhaled loudly. "His daughter? Why am I only hearing about a daughter now?"

"His wife, she is dead. He has a young girl," said the investigator.

The Brit huffed and puffed in exasperation. "And where is she?"

"I don't know," said the Belgian, and I breathed in, with relief. "But I can find out."

"Then do it." The Brit was over-elaborately calm, containing himself. "If this bloody Commando disappears again, things will get very uncomfortable you."

"I will deal with it," said the investigator.

"Get off the line," barked the Brit, and the investigator vanished.

"If he gets away in Boston," the Brit addressed the Professor, "I need you to get the rest of the circle, travel to Ireland and tidy things up. Immediately."

"But what about the Keeper?" said the Professor, "he's not authorised to allow anyone near the Heir between Beltane and Samhain."

I looked at Charity, who paused the recording, and lifted her shoulders to indicate she had no idea.

"It's Pagan shit," the twin broke in, reading from her iPhone. "The first one's about fertility, the second one's about... death and stuff." Charity cut her off by pressing play.

"Leave the Keeper to me," the Brit said. "I have a job for him. I'll make sure he's not around."

The Professor wasn't happy. "The Irish police – how do we navigate that?"

"We have people where we need them. You know that. You just get done what needs to be done." The Professor nodded, and the recording finished.

My heart hammered like a mortar drop.

*****

The Charity woman looked at me. "Is your daughter safe?"

"I don't know," I said.

"When did your wife die?"

"Just before I met you," I told her.

"You never said," her delivery was gentle now, his sister's less so.

"Umm, sorry to butt in like, but, we have an issue here. There was a new recording cracked, remember? So maybe we should, like, watch it?"

Charity came-to. She fumbled around, bringing up the fresh film. It had a real sense of urgency. The Brit was shouting. "So where is he now?"

"He's leaving my office building," the Professor replied. He was deferential. Little wonder, given the eruption his response had conjured from the Brit.

"To go where?" the Brit screamed, the sound distorting.

We appeared to be watching the video call the professor had made immediately after I had confronted him in New York. "I don't know," the professor began to shake his head in panic.

"Well, hadn't you better find out?" boomed the Brit, top right.

"Is OK," interjected the investigator. "We can pick him up, is no problem."

"But I thought you said he was dumping his phones?" the Brit blurted out in frustration.

"Oh, I am not watching his cell phone," shrugged the French-sounding bloke. "Phones are good, but not reliable, really. They are sometimes discarded, or, broken, and many people know they are compromised." There was flippancy to his delivery, which suggested complete confidence in his ability to find me.

"So how can you be sure you can track him?" asked the professor.

"Same as before," said the European, "he has one thing with him always."

"Which is?" yelled the Brit.

The European snorted. "Look, I do not ask who you are or what you do. I provide this service, and track the persons of interest to you. You have no need to know how I do this."

The Brit was silent for a moment. He had the tremor of an incendiary on the cusp of detonation. Then, his face loomed large in the screen, as he leaned in.

"Listen to me, you little Belgian bastard," he spat. "Do you think we can't find people ourselves? The only reason we chose you is because we don't have anyone in Ireland. We know everything about you. Your little rental home on Achill Island. Where your wife works, where your children go to school. You are not indispensable, you little shit."

The Belgian's eyes were wide. He was completely blindsided.

The Brit's voice gathered volume. "If you cross me, we will fuck-you-up. Do you understand that, or shall I speak more slowly!"

The Belgian sat still for a moment, evidently dumbfounded that he had been rumbled on the tech front.

"Now. What is it? The thing that the commando has with him all of the time?" The Brit paced his delivery, making each word crystal clear.

The Belgian's eyes fell. "He has the key to his boat," he replied, softly.

I felt the sister's head hit the back of my car seat as the charity woman paused the recording, and turned to face me. The twin groaned from the rear. Now I knew why Mini Marine's boffin hadn't detected anything. I had walked off the marina pontoon for lunch, with the tracker in my trousers.

"Tell me it's not in your pocket now, Sam," said the twin.

It was in my pocket.

"Ok," said the charity woman. "We need to get out of here."

"We need to get away from him," said the twin, incredulous.

"I need to know what else is on those recordings," I said.

"Eh, yeah," said the twin sarcastically, "that's the priority, yeah. Not that a bunch of – who knows what –looking to kill us."

I worked through the sequencing, and realised that they'd lost me in New York, because my boat keys had been bundled in my kit and flown home by Federal Express. But I'd picked the keys up again just that morning, and as such I'd handed them my whereabouts again.

I looked up. We were sitting in the part of the car park where articulated lorry drivers hauled in to get some sleep. Nobody was looking at us; they were all trying to appease their tachometers by lying in their curtained bunks. I watched a small dog pad over, a fluffy little yoke. In the distance two children swung a dog lead and played in the grass. The little pooch began to piddle against the rear wheel. I gently opened the door, and held out my hand. The dog came over and licked it. I grabbed it by the scruff and hauled it into the car. Then I took the boat keys, both the padlock key and the plastic-encased engine isolator, and rammed them down the dog's gullet. It yelped and whined, and I could see the children turn in the distance. The dog coughed a little, then struggled to get away from me. Satisfied that it was down and staying down, I let the dog out the door. The Belgian would have fun tracking that.

The twin was obviously working through the logic of the recordings too. I could see her shaking her head. "You actually met this bloke?" she said. "This Professor?"

"Two days ago. In Manhattan," I said.

"So, we need to go to the police, in the north maybe, get him picked up?" said the sister.

"Afraid not," I said. "He's dead."

It was now plain how monumental an indulgence killing the Professor had been. I'd missed an opportunity to round up his group at that bloody apartment in Belfast. I doubted anyone would go near it now, in the middle of a police investigation.

"Eh, what?" The sister was struggling with news of his death, and was shouting.

"He killed himself. Long story."

"Unbelievable."

"How long until the next recording is cracked?" I asked her.

"Depends on how long it is," she said.

If the Belgian was looking for Isla, I needed to find the Belgian. I started the car, and began to pull off.

"Oh, so we're going with you now, are we?" the sister said, her voice thick with Dublin attitude.

"We need to get to Achill Island," I said.

"We're safer with him for the moment Sis, honestly." The charity woman had her head turned to the back seat. "I've seen him working, we're probably better off with him."

"I'm not going to the West of Ireland with ye," barked the sister. "You can let me out now."

I swerved to the hard shoulder; I'd had enough of her.

"No, no, no, Sis, we stay together," said Charity. "They know who we are and probably where we live. The only way to sort it is to deal with them. Sam can deal with them."

"The Guards can deal with them!" yelled the twin.

"You heard the man, the cops are 'on board.' Let's get away from here. If they've tracked him this far, we need to keep moving."

I looked in the rear-view mirror. "Get out if you're getting out. Otherwise the next stop is Achill Island," I said to the twin.

She slumped down petulantly, her arms folded across her chest. I took that as confirmation, pulled into the traffic, and headed West.

*****

Some people love barren, but it's not for me. Bogland represents one long, turgid reminder of freezing, wet nights yomping across vacuous countryside, the mud clinging to my boots, the earth trying to lay premature claim to my sodden, aching, carcass. Those months of training for the Marines, and then the SBS, were far from fun. Nor was the drive to County Mayo fun. I was tailgating, speeding, and hurtling ahead, despite the swearing and gasps from my passengers, who clearly thought that I was destined to cause their deliverance. We swept through the flat, black gorse brush, Heaney's turf, where Ireland's brutal history was embalmed, and concealed.

In the past, I'd sailed by Achill Island, but I'd never been on it. Neither had my passengers. The twin, with her Google maps and her iPhone, became my consultant. At least it gave her purpose beyond criticising my driving.

"There's not much there," she said, "there's like some villages and a good few pubs, mostly holiday cottages. And a beach."

"What about access?" I asked. I hadn't a clue whether getting to the island involved a ferry.

"Well, far as I can see there's one bridge, but that's all. It looks pretty tight." She looped her phone around the headrest and I glanced at it, then she made the image bigger. I grunted. That seemed like good news.

"See where the broadband connection is best," I scrabbled around for ideas about how to locate the Belgian. I reckoned he'd need pretty good bandwidth in his line of work. She began tapping away.

"Seems ok in the villages," she said. "But I'd say he's not hard-wired – that's too volatile. I'd say he uses a dish out there, for when the electric goes down in winter."

The twin may have been a pain in the arse, but her reasoning and skills were on the money. We passed a small supermarket close to the bridge, and I decided there was no point in wasting time. I pulled over, and turned to Charity.

"Can you take a screen shot of the Belgian from the iPad, and enlarge it?" She shook her head to indicate her technical incompetence.

"Here, give it to me," said the twin, and I heard the sound of a camera shutter. She handed the iPad into the front again, job done.

"Right," I said to Charity, reasoning that she was the most likely to get the desired response. "Can you go inside and ask where he lives?"

"I can try," she said. "But they'll think I'm a cop."

I didn't care what they thought. They could either tell her nicely, or have me wreck the place.

She returned fifteen minutes later, during which time I had twice considered the strangulation of her sister, as she banged on about the mess I had dragged them into.

"Sorry, took a bit of plamasing."

I looked at her quizzically.

"Sweet-talking," explained her know-it-all sister.

"He lives in Keel, up a hill. I have rough directions but they only go so far."

There's windswept, and there's ravaged, and I couldn't work out whether the village was beautiful, or battered. We tore around the place, up lanes and roads, until the place we were looking for presented itself. At the back of one falling-down house loomed a dish NASA would have been proud of. I wondered what the locals thought the little Belgian was up to in there. I didn't bother with a soft approach. I parked hard, wedging his Jeep in, told the women to stay put, and didn't break stride as my shoulder hit his front door. The whole frame gave way.

Inside there was a scuffling as someone took off, but it was useless. He could tear into the surrounding terrain, but it was home away from home for me, and he wouldn't get away. I caught him wrestling with a broken PVC door at the back, and used my forearm to pin his face against the glass, and to raise his feet off the floor. His lips slabbered the windowpane, his heavy panting condensed against it, and in that moment, something came to me. It was as if I'd taken a round in the trunk, it nearly took the legs from me, but I had to remain standing. I had to see this part through, before I reasoned out the rest.

"You've been looking for me," I whispered into his ear. "So, hi. Here I am."

"He's choking Sam, put him down." Charity was at my back. But I couldn't shake the knowledge that the Belgian had volunteered my daughter as leverage, and I wanted to damage him.

"You might need the little shit," I heard the twin say, as he began to expire. She was right. I dropped him.

Ten minutes later we were sitting in a studio, surrounded by monitors and stacks of servers, cables pouring out like meat from a mincer. Lots of little dots flashing.

"Cool," said the twin, admiring the Belgian's set up. I gave her a look. She reciprocated, with interest.

"You've a choice to make," I told him, and he rubbed the back of his head and looked up at me in fear. "You tell us what we want to know, or, in return for you betraying my child, I kill you."

Charity was looking everywhere but at me, or him. It probably dawned on her what she had commissioned in the past.

"If I help you, *they* will kill me," he said, which sounded like a reasonable assumption.

"Well, if you give me enough information, I'll deal with them," which was all starting to sound a bit ridiculous, but at that point, it was exactly what I intended to do. In any case, he had little choice, die now, or die later.

"Just tell him, please," Charity pleaded. She had heart, and had evidently inherited the compassion gene in the womb.

Her less sensitive sister was already playing with the computers. "I reckon I could give this a crack if you want to just do him," she told me.

I leaned forward and caught him by the hair and began to drag him towards the door of his den.

"Please no," said Charity. Between the sisters, they made a bloody convincing pair.

"Ok, ok, ok," he screamed, "ok ok."

I gave him a kick, and dragged him up to his desk. It half encircled him. I leaned forward to speak into his ear. "If, at any point, you tell me a lie, I will make sure that this 'circle' knows where I got my information from. Some of the questions I am about to ask, I know the answers to. Some I do not. If at any point you piss me around, I let her do the work," I nodded my head at the twin, "and then you and I will take a walk, OK?"

"I'm not for fucking around," he said, "I get it, I get it."

"Who is the American?" I said.

"He is dip-lo-mat," he said, "he, umm, makes business for Nortzen Ireland, for econ-om-y," he said. I found his delivery mildly irritating. He'd been clearer on the recordings. Perhaps it was the fear.

"Where is he from?" I asked, establishing his commitment to the truth, as old agent handlers had taught us, years before.

"He is not so important," said the Belgian. "He is academique, from Boston. He is living in New York."

"Who is the Englishman?" I asked, expecting a quick answer.

The Belgian looked terrified. "Whish Englishman?" he said, his eyes fluttering all over the place.

"This one, you fucknuckle," the twin said, thrusting the iPad in front of him. His jaw muscles clamped when he saw the screen grab from the recording.

"I donno," he muttered. "I not joking you, I do not know who he is."

"But you know *where* he is don't you?" said the twin, who seemed to me to be making a better job of this than I was. The Belgian gently rocked his head as if to say, maybe, maybe not.

"You had a hook-up with him. You have the kit here to trace his IP, or at least the one he used for the call."

Again, the Belgian remained silent, staring up at her with real fear in his eyes.

"I'll find it myself," she said, turning to the middle of two keyboards, and hammering away.

The Belgian leaned forward to begin protest. He evidently didn't like the idea of someone looking through his files, particularly when his system appeared to be live, and therefore open to interrogation.

But the Brit wasn't my main concern. "What about my daughter?" I asked him.

He turned to me, and cowered at the same time, like a dog that knew it was about to be get the stick. "The Englishman has made arrangements to send someone to find her," he said.

"Who?" I shouted.

"The Keeper, they call him," said the Belgian. "But," he held up his hands, "I don't know, I don't, I don't know," he was emphasizing every word, "who this Keeper is."

I believed him.

"Where has he been sent?" I asked.

"All I find was your parents' phones register to a mast. They make no calls and they do not answer calls."

"Where!?" I screamed at him.

"L'Estartit," he said, ducking his head as if expecting a slap.

"France?" I inquired, genuinely shocked.

"No, is Spain."

The twin was working on one of the other keyboards. "Costa Brava," she said. "Very nice. Your folks, they must be using some pretty old devices, yeah?" she asked.

"They don't have smartphones," I confirmed.

She pulled up a map on a screen. "You didn't get very close did ye?" she turned to the Belgian, then back to the screen. "Sim-based tracking is pretty shitty," she said. "He only got to within a few miles."

Which seemed far too bloody close for me.

"So, when was the Keeper sent?" I rounded on the Belgian.

"Three hours ago," he said.

I made to leave, but two things occurred to me.

"These women will be needing your Jeep," I said. "Get all you can from that computer, then destroy everything," I told the twin.

"OK," she tuned back to the screen. I looked at Charity.

"I'll leave you a rucksack. There's a grand sterling in it. Get yourself somewhere safe, and I'll send you an e-mail when all this is sorted."

She had the countenance of a car wreck.

"You," I looked at the Belgian, "where was the Englishman's IP? Where was he, when he dialled in?"

"I have it here," said the twin.

When I looked at the screen, I understood why he was so terrified.

Twenty-Four

Three hours was a hell of a head start, particularly given that I was four hours' drive away from the Dublin airport. Depending on what flight he caught, that gave the Keeper as much as seven hours' grace, but I had three things in my favour. I knew my parents' habits, I had a friend called Mini Marine, and I would know the Keeper when I saw him.

I cursed myself for not getting Charity or her sister to book me a flight before I left Achill Island. I then debated whether to stop and buy a phone, or to push ahead and get to Dublin airport. In any event, I badly needed fuel, but the bloody garage didn't sell mobile phones.

Three hours and twenty minutes later I abandoned the hire car in the same spot where I'd fought with a pimp almost one year before, and ran into Terminal One. I scoured the departure screen for a flight to Spain, and racked my over-exhausted brain for a sense of the geography. There was a flight to Barcelona, which seemed like a good option, and another to Girona, but I had no idea where that was. The woman at the Ryanair desk showed me a map, and I paid in cash.

Seven hours and forty minutes after I left Achill, I stood in the warm heat of Girona Airport. It was dinky, but it had everything I needed, including cars for hire with integral GPS. Twenty miles later I had set up a Spanish sim pay-as-you-go cell phone. Dog-tired, I called my old base at Faslane, and asked for Mini.

"Where have you been, pal? I've been trying to reach ye."

"I had to ditch my old phone, Min."

"Y'lright?" Western Scots, like the Irish, manage to weld all their words into one.

"Yes, mate, how did you get on with tracking my folks?"

"Aye, we have them. They're in a Spanish toon near the Iles de Medes."

"LEstartit?" I cut in.

"Aye?" He sounded surprised. "You're way ahead of me are ye, Sam?"

"I'm less than an hour's drive from there as we speak. I need a fix though, Min." He could hear the desperation in my voice.

His voice lowered, and became softer, apologetic, "They're no GPS phones, pal."

"Min, I know, just give me your best, please."

"Looks like a wee peninsula, round the corner from a beach, kind of private like." He began to sound frustrated and I could almost see him shaking his head. "It's about a mile long, and there's coast to the east so no masts at sea to triangulate for sure. The phones hav'nie moved in hours, mebbe even days."

He read me the co-ordinates he had, and I punched them into the GPS.

"Thanks Min. Really mate, thank you."

"Let me know how you get on, when you can, like."

As I drove, I debated calling the Spanish police, but I didn't know what I could say to them. Two Irish adults, one child, at risk from an unidentified person? Can't tell you who, can't say whether that the person is definitely even there. Can't tell you who I am, or anything about the background. Can't even speak Spanish. Besides, the real issue nagging at me was what would happen afterwards? Think ahead Sam, I told myself. It's not just the next move, it's the move after that.

If the Spanish plods did manage to arrest the Keeper, I would become material to a case that could not be proven. That would mean Isla and I would never have peace, because I'd know the truth. The Brit's location when he made the hook-up calls confirmed a nagging fear, and I knew that if the Keeper made it into custody, he would be protected. The Circle would not rest until the evidence, i.e. me, was destroyed, which would make an orphan of Isla. I chewed the whole situation over for so long that I arrived in L'Estartit before I'd made up my mind.

The GPS took me through a bustling little town, shortly after siesta time. My impatience was pointless. Nothing would move more quickly for my frustration, so I zoomed in on the little screen, took a mental map of the peninsula Min had referred to, abandoned the car, and started running.

I glared into the face of every person I passed. I listened for the three voices most familiar to me, as I raced past the restaurants and bars. Awnings were being wound out, and tables set for evening service. I prayed like I'd never prayed before, that my Mum would be following her usual routine.

I must have stood out like a snowman on a beach as I
raced through the town, while everyone else sauntered at a
retirement pace. Life in L'Estartit was obviously generous.
Nobody showed any urgency. I began to panic that I'd become
disorientated, as I had been expecting to see the masts of
a boat marina before now, but as usual, the flat visual of the
map confused the actual size of the place. Eventually, I saw
the tips of rigging as I emerged from a pedestrian street, and
kept heading towards the rocks. I was adding things up in
my head; the previous flight had been from Belfast, an extra
two hours' drive from Dublin for the Keeper. That made him
three, maybe four hours ahead of me. But for all he knew, I
was still in Ireland, and I was banking on his lack of urgency
to see me through.

I ran along a road, about five feet above a short beach.
My parents are predictable in some ways. They like a drink
in the evening, just one, before dinner, and they like to feel
like they've earned it. That might involve a walk, some work
in the garden, or when the sun is on their backs, a swim in
the sea. I scoured the sand for them, but it was crowded
with broad white floppy hats, and broad white floppy British
bellies. They'll not go for that, I reckoned. They like their
space. So I kept running.

Beyond the sand there appeared to be a road that rose
slightly, and curled around a bend. Above and to my left were
apartments, beautifully appointed, stylish, with generous
sun covers and sand shutters. I wondered if the phones
were sitting inside, on a table, charging merrily. I closed out
notions of the three people I cared about most, lying face
down, dead upon the marble floors.

That image made me desperate, as I hammered up the
incline, cursing myself for believing that I would find them
alive and well. My legs began to burn and slow as the

optimism wore off, and I cast around more in desperation than confidence. The place was all but deserted, apart from two local kids clambering onto bikes at a bridge, their day fishing off the rocks evidently over. I grabbed the timber railing and lowered my head between by shoulders to catch my breath. My chest heaved, and I became acutely aware of my increasing vintage, my lack of energy, and my fear. I looked up slowly, the sweat steaming my vision.

And then I saw her.

She was standing, with a plastic rake, in her swimsuit and crocs, less then forty feet below me. She looked amazingly happy, and brown, and was pottering about with sand stuck all over her. I hunted for my parents, and saw a woman swimming in the cove further below. I could tell by the stroke it was Mum, chin high, short, strong strokes. Then I found my dad, in his shorts and sandals, twenty feet to the right of Isla. The relief would have been enormous, if he hadn't been standing there talking to the Keeper.

                              **

It was a desperate situation. Dad, as usual, was just shooting the breeze with what he must have thought was a fellow Irishman abroad. He would not have given a second thought to the fact that the man was wearing city shoes in a rocky cove, or that he had jeans on and a fleece round his waist, despite the heat being above 30 degrees Celsius.

I was too far gone, and made yet another mistake. Had I managed to get some proper sleep in the preceding week, things might have worked out better.

My approach was too fast. I don't know to this day whether it was excitement or desperation that took me down that rocky cove, but it was stupid beyond words. I skipped over the rocks, and bounded and slid down the incline. I should have predicted Isla' reaction; she looked up and became over-joyed.

'Daddy!' she yelled, thrilled. Then confusion crossed her face, as I ignored her completely and made for her grandfather and the man beside him.

My dad looked up then, and began to form a baffled smile, and then realised something was very, very wrong. I was still too far away when the Keeper turned to face me. He immediately and with determination reached for the pocket of his fleece. I screamed out. 'Dad, get out of the way!'

But dads are dads, no matter what age they are. And children are more important to them than anything, no matter how old *they* might be. My father realised that the man he'd been chatting to was no friend, and as the Keeper produced a short knife, my dad reached to grab his arm. And then I heard Dad wretch, exhaling as if throwing up.

Dad took the puncture to the chest, but he didn't let go of the Keeper. His protective instincts gave his old arms strength, returning to them the gorilla-like power he'd had when he was my age. I saw his enormous freckled forearms lock around the keeper's wrist and elbow, gripping him as he tried to wrestle the knife free.

I had no choice; I had to flatten them together. I left the surface about eight feet above where they stood, and hit them mid-ships, toppling them down onto the sharp rocks below. The fall could have done as much damage to my dad as the knife wound. I have never seen a cove so jagged.

I never wanted Isla to witness another death. I never wanted her to see another violent act. Her recovery from the death of her mother was far from complete, and yet here she was on the cusp of watching her grandfather die too.

Dad was panting to my left, reaching for air, but God bless him, he still had his hands around the Keeper's wrist. I grabbed the free arm and twisted it backwards to open the assailant's rib cage, then fell on it with my knees.

It felt like time paused as I wrenched him around and stared into the shock of his eyes. Under me, terrified, was the Counsellor.

I took both his ears, lifted his head, and smashed his skull onto the rocks beneath him.

**

I was patching Dad's entry wound when the Counsellor came-to. I already knew what I was going to do with him. Isla was in a desperate state, heaving with tears and wanting to hug me, but I was quickly soaked in dad's blood as I worked on him. Mum was a star, having cut her feet to slices by tearing from the sea, and running up the rocks. She was as calm as Dad had been, and saw the sense in keeping Isla turned away, while doing exactly what I asked of her, to keep Dad alive.

"Daddy, stop shouting at Granny," Isla said, as I barked directions at her.

There was a puncture in his left lung for sure, but the sticky flap from a pack of wet wipes allowed me to make sure it didn't fill with blood, and drown him. By placing the flap above the entry wound, it acted like a draught excluder, sucking flat to the chest on the breath in, but blowing out to allow the exhale. There was no catastrophic bleed. The messiest wound was on the back of his head from the fall, so I packed that, and then turned to the Counsellor.

I found his phone in the pocket of the fleece, and handed it to Mum, who has great Spanish, and knew exactly where we were. I couldn't put Dad over my shoulder because of the wound in his chest, and when I lifted him, he even managed to speak. "It's OK, I can walk son."

I laughed at that, but I appreciated his hardiness. The tough never show the depth of their resolve until it is required. It was a lesson I'd learned during Marines selection in Devon, and again later with the SBS in Poole. The most gentle of people often turned out to be the ones who not only survived, but who pulled the others through, when the going got tight. I prayed Dad's age would not overcome his gristle.

Mum, too, was unbelievable. Isla was far too heavy for a woman her age. Regardless, Mum swept her up and with a piggyback and in bare feet, took her to the bridge. There I laid Dad, and explained what needed to happen. "You're not going to like this, but it's the only way," I said to Mum.

Isla stared up at me, and I addressed her first.

"Look wee love, you need to listen to me really, really carefully ok?"

Her big eyes were still filled up with fluid, and she nodded.

"I have to leave you..."

"No, Daddy," she cried.

"Just for a little while, I promise. Not like last time, not for days and days. Just for as long as a movie, ok? Just for as long as Ghostbusters. I pinkie promise."

Her little finger became smeared in her grandfather's blood. In the distance, I could hear the distressed whoop of an emergency vehicle. Isla nodded to me. I turned to Mum.

"This attack happened on the rocks. You were approached by some mugger who saw you guys alone. He stabbed Dad, and ran off. He didn't get anything. Don't let Isla out of your sight. Take her into the interview booth if you have to. Don't let any plod talk to her on her own. She's on holiday with you. Tell them you have called me and that I am on my way from Ireland."

"What are you going to do?"

I looked at Isla, but didn't want to say anything that she could regurgitate in front of anyone. I whispered in Mum's ear. "I need to deal with yer man," I nodded below to the rocks. "He's Irish, and he came far too close."

She just looked at me in stunned silence, and eventually nodded, and posed another question. "So, are we ok then, there's nobody else to worry about?"

She was asking whether the Counsellor was working alone, which was something I hadn't considered. My instincts told me that he was flying solo.

"Yes. How will I find you? Afterwards like?" I asked her.

"There's only one hospital round here," she said. "We had to take your dad there last week for an ear infection."

Which explained why he hadn't been swimming.

"Ok, I'll find it. Stay there till I join you. Have you money? You'll need clothes."

"They're in the bag down there," she nodded to the cove. "I'll ask the police to bring them to us, when they arrive."

I hugged Dad, whose breathing was steady-ish, and looked at the two women, in their swimsuits and the blood. I kissed Isla and told her not to tell anyone that she had seen me, and not to talk to the police, and then I leapt over the railing and hopped down the rocks once more.

**

Dragging the Counsellor into the sea was easy. He was still unconscious, and I worried that he might die. His breath was laboured, and as I rested his head against my chest to swim him out, I could feel the gristle and bone of skull fragments rub against my shirt. We swam tight to the rocks towards a jutting headland. I reckoned that it was so steep that it would be almost impossible for anyone to see us from above. There was virtually no wash, and I was thankful for the negligible tidal pull of the Mediterranean.

Once we reached the outcrop, I found a small, shelved inlet. It was not quite a cave, but it was covered and impenetrable by land. I paddled us in, and used the Counsellor's arms to wedge his mouth above water, Christ-like, his head hanging between his shoulders, his arms spread above. The water around us gradually filled with his blood, as I gently trod water, preserving as much energy as possible. I had a long haul ahead.

When darkness was established, I swam out around the headland, and looked for a vessel of some sort. Of course, there was nothing. Well, save for a few hundred yachts and motor cruisers sitting elegantly in the marina. However, twenty feet beyond, their owners were cavorting merrily in the restaurants and bars which embroidered the harbour. The way my luck was going, I would be sure to steal a boat owned by someone within spitting distance of the theft. Regardless, I swam towards the lights.

One option presented itself, so with reluctance, I took it. Lashed to the stanchions on the leeward side of a fifty-foot ketch, was a broad stand-up paddleboard. The long stock of its oar was within reach, tied to the toe-rail. I didn't dare to stand up on it as I left the marina, shoving it instead, like a learner swimmer might push a float. Once out of the immediate sight of the revellers, I clambered on top. It wasn't until I dipped the blade in the water that the penny finally dropped about how stupid I had been.

Feet together, with the water gently lapping over my toes, I realised how the intruder had got on board our boat. There was no way the radar would have picked up the polystyrene core of a surfboard like the one beneath my feet, or indeed, the plastic paddle. I had seen SUPs being used a thousand times. Why it had never occurred to me before was a total mystery.

I ducked under the shelf as I entered the cove, but I could see nothing. I knew where I'd left the Counsellor, crucifixional in the depth of the half-cave. I dropped to my knees, the blade under my groin, and paddled like a dog, hands immersed on either side of the board. It butted against the rocks, but the Counsellor was gone.

I almost panicked. Worst-case scenario was that he had fallen forwards, and drowned. I dropped into the water, now breath-robbingly frigid, and thrashed about beneath the surface, but it was pointless. I couldn't see anything. My head swam with the adverse scenarios his death posed. An Irishman, stabbed. Another Irishman washed up close by, with serious head wounds. A third Irishman, with a colourful career history, flies in before – not after – the stabbing, but claims to have arrived as a result *of* it. I had to find him.

I got back on the board and paddled out of the cove again, imagining what the Counsellor was likely to have done, had he been able to escape. The gentle swell would not have prevented him turning either right, towards the marina, or left, towards the scene of the stabbing. He had no reason to swim to sea, and I assumed he had simply slipped beneath the surface and died. I hoped against hope that he had not.

I reckoned he would hit for help and so I turned right, powering the paddle into the water and driving forward. I was surprised at the speed of the board, and used the reflection and illumination of the town's lights to scour the rock face and the sea ahead, for signs of a swimmer. The paddle's displacement made a plunge and ripple sound as it cut through the surface, gliding the board like a skimming stone, straight as an arrow. The noise helped me catch a break.

"Help, please!" I heard a weak call to my right. There was still a mile between the town and me, and I couldn't see anyone, but the voice seemed to come from the rock face. It was unmistakably Irish.

"Ola?" I called, hoping he would guide me towards him.

"Over here," he called.

I was upon him before I finally saw what was happening. The Counsellor was hanging like a gymnast from a rock, faced into the cliff, and unable to see me approach. He heard me though, because he kept muttering.

"Here, please, por favour, over here."

The logistics of this were not ideal. I needed him compliant, but I needed him alive. I also needed to get him onto the board. Nothing easy about any of that, particularly given that he was hanging off a rock and was likely to go boogaloo when he saw his would-be saviour.

I sat on my arse, my shins dangling in the water for stability, and manoeuvred the board parallel to the rock face. Then I placed my hand upon his shoulder.

"Ok, ok, ok," I said, reassuringly, then crooked my elbow around his throat and began to choke him. His thrashing did not begin immediately. He evidently thought he was being rescued, but when it did dawn upon him, he nearly capsized the board with his kicking.

It took three full minutes of careful squeezing and release. I had to make sure the pressure was even, and just enough to knock him out without causing brain damage. It was the second time he'd been rendered unconscious that day, and I knew that I was very lucky not to have killed him on the previous occasion.

I lumped him onto the board, face down in a jury-rigged recovery position. Placing one foot between his legs, and the other on the small of his back, I started digging deep with the paddle. His body made the board less predictable as it wobbled beneath me, but we had a long way to go, and I was out of alternatives.

I estimated the Isles de Medes to be about one mile offshore. Everything I knew about them had come from an article I'd read on the in-flight magazine, and I'd been so distracted, that I didn't remember much. The Medes Islands had been fortified at various times. I recalled mention of Napoleon, and of the fact that the Isles were now part of a protected nature reserve, which suited me just fine. What really interested me though was that the article had mentioned underwater caves.

Almost an hour later I sculled around to the southeast side of the rocks, the sheer height of which offered few opportunities for landing. I'd seen an image in the article of divers bobbing merrily just off an outcrop, but in the half-light, it took a bit of finding. Once there I dragged the board and the Counsellor up onto the hard ground, and laid him face down. Then I placed my head on the small of his back, and fell asleep, assured that he could not get away again without me knowing it.

*****

I have no idea how long I slept, but it was black dark when the Counsellor began to shift. I lifted my head and regarded his pathetic progress. He shuffled on the rock face, then moaned and sobbed, reaching around, trying to work out where he was. I let him scrabble for a while, deliberating on how to get from him what I needed. He wasn't even aware of my presence until I spoke.

"Scream if you want to, nobody can hear you. Might be best to get it out."

I heard him scuttle around on all fours, then halt, stock-still, like a lizard, his senses sharpened. I waited as his mind reeled. "Sam?" he said eventually.

"Yes," I said. "Although you're not supposed to know my name, are you?"

He grunted. I couldn't make out his expression.

"I know about the circle," I began, "the Harvard Professor, the Heir, and your relationship with her."

He paused, computing. "How?"

"The mirror. In your bathroom."

"What?" he spat, incredulous.

"When we spoke in there. I ran the shower, to distort any listening devices."

"You bugged me?"

"No. Do try to keep up," I said, aiming to pile on the confusion and consolidate control. "The steam clung to the mirror. It showed me that her face had been pressed against it. Her scar, all down her face."

His breathing became silent. "You've met her, the Heir?"

"Not yet."

"But the scar?" he was thinking hard, trying to work out how I knew.

"You told me about it, without meaning to. You touched your face when you talked about her being cut. But the steamed mirror showed it to me. Your hand, beside her head. Your other one probably pressed against her skull. You behind her. All to yourself. No sick circle looking on. Just you. Raping her, abusing her."

"Not rape!" he spat, angrily, shuffling about and rising on his knees.

In truth, it hadn't clicked with me until I'd forced the Belgian's face against his back door, his breath condensing on the glass.

"You can call it what you like," I told the Counsellor. "You probably think you're in a relationship. Next thing, you'll be telling me you love her." I poured scorn into my delivery.

"I *do* love her. She and I, we are together."

"That," I said, "I do believe. You wanted to get her away from the others. You wanted them to stop raping her. You were jealous."

"No. I was protecting her."

"You're not her counsellor, you're her Keeper," I said. "You're one of the circle. You are its master of hounds. But you got jealous of them, having their twisted way with her."

"She loves me," he said.

"Have you never heard of Stockholm syndrome?"

"She loves me. I was getting her out of it," he repeated.

"'After how many years of abusing her? '" I asked. "'She used you. And you, her jailer, saw a way to get her out. Through me."

I heard him roll off his knees and onto his arse.

I looked in his direction. "It took a while to work out what you were up to. Why would one of the circle bring in a mercenary like me, to investigate the abuse?"

"I love her," was all he said.

"You thought you could play me against them, didn't you? You thought that you could persuade me that you were her shrink, nothing more, and that I would find them and kill them, and then you would take her as your own."

"You make it sound like I'm as bad as them."

"You're no better. You fed me just enough information to lead me to the members of the Circle. The Boston barman. The old woman in Dublin. You killed her, too, didn't you?"

I took his silence as acceptance.

"You calculated that I would kill them all, and that by telling them I was coming after them, you could get permission to move the Heir away, ready for your new life, your escape. Poor bloody woman."

"She needed someone to free her. There was no other way. Just, no other way," he stressed.

"But you were one of them from the start. You were an abuser, a rapist, a sick fanatic. Did you really think that you'd be able to sail off into the sunset with her? Your victim?"

"I was trying to save her," he said.

"Were you trying to save her when you came for my family?" I asked.

"It's not that simple," he said.

"I know. You're afraid of someone. Someone who has played you, who knows who all of you are, who can destroy your fantasy life with the Heir."

It was then that he began to sob. I kept on the heat. "Did you cut her too? Did you put that scar on her face? Did you skin her feet when she was small? Did you rape her as a child?"

It was all I could do to stop myself from striking him again. I waited for a long time. "There is only one way you will ever see her again," I told him.

"How?" he asked, suspicious.

"I need to know about the others. The Brit who has you so terrified. The hierarchy, the arrangements. I need to finish what you started."

He said nothing for a few minutes.

And then he talked, and talked.

And then I reminded myself that he had come to kill my daughter. And so he was introduced to an underwater cave, and I paddled ashore to see my dad.

*****

The going wasn't easy. The key to my hire car had become saturated, so I took out the small, rear triangular window to unlock the back door manually. That triggered the alarm, which woke the locals at 7 a.m. The key in the ignition stopped the siren. There were three notices crammed behind the windshield wipers, all of which appeared to be parking fines. At least the wheel hadn't been clamped.

Contrary to what Mum had said, there seemed to be a dozen hospitals in the area. Most of them were small and privately owned, and it took far too long for me to realise that my definition of a hospital, and that of the Spanish, were totally different. Eventually I spotted an elderly man clutching a freshly baked baguette, who not only spoke English but *was* English. He told me that the nearest hospital with an emergency department was in Palamos, half an hour's drive from L'Estartit.

A nurse looked at me with suspicion. I was still damp in places, from the paddle, but at least the blood had washed away. I was salty, for sure, and must have looked pretty haggard. The nurse may have put it down to a long flight; I didn't really care, until I saw Isla and my mum. My daughter's little feet were brown, save from the straps of some beach shoes she must have been given. A blanket lay on the floor, and her little legs were curled up towards her chest, as her head lay across her Granny's lap. My mum was dozing upright in a chair, not really asleep, but not awake either. Two feet away, Dad was propped up on pillows upon the ramp of a bed, a tube out of his nose, packing around his chest, a drip in his arm and a ventilator billowing away at his side. His heart was being monitored; it looked steady to my untrained eye.

The room was private, and even had its own shower and toilet. Mum and Isla were dressed for the beach; the police had evidently retrieved their bag. I put one hand on Dad's shoulder, and took his enormous paw in mine. He stirred, and his crusty eyes cracked open. When he saw me, he smiled, and then closed his eyes in peace for longer than was comfortable.

Then he opened them again. His chest heaved with effort. "Ok pal," was all he managed, the plastic mask steaming up as he spoke.

"Hi Dad."

There was no point in asking how he was doing. I could see it all. He was alive, and with the exception of infection, he ought to be ok.

"She's been so good," my mum spoke from behind me. "Isla held his hand all night."

I turned to look at her, as her eyes welled up.

"What does the doctor say?" I nodded towards Dad.

"Punctured lung," she said. "There was cardiac arrest last night, which was terrifying, but they got him back in the ambulance and he's been stable since."

The guilt was enormous, but mum didn't have time for recrimination. Everyone, including me, was ok, and that was good enough for her. "I'm not going to ask what this is all about," she said. "But is it over?"

I walked over and scooped up my daughter, and hugged her in tight. She stirred awake.

"Almost," I said. "Almost."

Twenty-Five

Westminster is stunning, even to those with little regard for what happens inside. I'd been there before countless times, on close protection duty, which I hated. Perhaps that's why I had no time for the people who occupied the green and red benches inside. Perhaps it was because of my pals, led by such fools, who had died in the dirt and the dust of distant lands.

Of course, there had to be good among the bad, but I was searching for the latter. I had run through the scenarios time and again; the recce, the surveillance, the approach, the ending. In any event, none of it was necessary.

I picked him up as he emerged from the Palace, no doubt having signed in for the day to claim his cash. Peers could take a daily allowance, money for nothing, if they so chose; the Brit couldn't have spent more than an hour inside. He certainly couldn't have taken his seat in the Lords' chamber. Then he hopped in a private car, some up-market taxi, and took off. So I got on the phone. "Where's he going?"

"Lemme see," said the Belgian, who I now had over a barrel. He had a vested interest in me ending the Circle, and a deep fear of its members finding out that he had talked. Between him and the bolshie twin, I had some pretty high-tech support. I listened to him type, as he scuttled around the Brit's diary, held on some server inside the building I was staring at. "Is good news," he said.

"Hurry up," I told him.

"He is going to Belfast."

So, I went too.

**

I had prepared for a showdown outside some exclusive London Gentleman's club. I imagined I'd be denied entry, that I would have to wait outside for the Brit to emerge, full of brandy and bravado. But Belfast isn't London.

The Belgian was able to tell me where the Brit was booked to stay, and where the taxi would deliver him the following day. I debated taking him at his hotel, but opted instead to use the hacked information to my advantage. I decided to wait, in the hope that his visit would lead me to others in the Circle.

Google got me there. To 4 Royal Avenue. The Ulster Reform Club. I had never heard of it, but I had passed the building a thousand times. Its website boasted partner establishments all over the world, but predominantly in London. Many were ex-military or naval organisations. The promotional images for the Reform Club gushed forth plush high-backed chairs, deep leather sofas, ornate casino tables and dark, stained timber floors. There was even a snooker and billiards room. Then I began to wonder what the Brit was up to, coming to Belfast. Posh as it was, someone like him couldn't compare the Reform Club to his own, old-boy establishment. It wasn't until I saw who he was meeting, that I realised. The Brit was looking for me.

*****

I stood in my suit, in my sweat, in astonishment, as my old Major walked down Royal Avenue. He stood out like a sore thumb, straight back, garish green tie, matching pocket-handkerchief. He looked every inch the English officer, parading down the street like he owned it, in his hand-stitched shoes. I had but a few moments to make a decision. In haste, I calculated what was happening.

The Brit was evidently digging around in my back catalogue. He had found the Major, who had nothing but loathing for me. There had been many successful operations in which he'd got the glory, and I'd got the scars, which had made him more bitter than grateful. The lines were more blurred between officers and ratings in the SBS. Sure, rank mattered, but less so than in the army, or the Marines.

Not to the Major though. He despised the fact that I'd had more of a relationship with my team than with the brass, like him. He hated the fact that I wouldn't tell him why I had gone AWOL after Gaza. It was he who had busted me back to the Marines after Jerusalem. He'd insisted that I was not to be trusted in Special Forces. Seeing him in Belfast summoned an anger in me, and I decided to take his place in the posh seats.

The options were few. I'd done what I could to conceal my identity. I'd acquired a beard in the preceding week, and I'd grabbed a hat before I left for town. It wasn't much, and to take a man out in broad daylight in a city centre is no straightforward proposition. Unlike most UK or Irish cities, Belfast people are less inclined to take a wide berth. If there is a scrap on the street, you can bet that strangers will back the underdog and wade in with the boots. Plus, the police are armed. Besides all that, brass or not, he was a Major in the Special Forces, and he knew how to handle himself.

I glanced down the alleyway between Primark and Tescos, right beside the Reform Club. There was a pub down there, but the laneway was busy. I knew what was at the end though, so I tried to suppress my temper and go for smarts.

Recognition scudded across his face like sunshine from under a cloud. He was nearly at the door of the club as I approached, my face open and smiling, my hand extended. He was confused. That suggested that he had indeed been invited to discuss me, and so my appearance was particularly alarming.

I extended my hand. I had to play this with complete confidence. "Thanks for coming Major," I said. "Sorry for all the cloak and dagger, necessary I'm afraid."

The Major stared at me. "What the bloody hell is going on, Ireland?" he said. At least his hostility was consistent.

"It's sensitive, Major. Our mutual friend has had to change the venue. Press, I'm afraid," I said. "Reporters, inside. Coincidental. They're there for another event. Nonetheless, not ideal."

"What?" he struggled.

"Look Sir, our peer friend was not able to discuss this on the telephone, so I suggested he mention me as a bit of a ruse, as it were, to persuade you to pop over from London. We had no way of knowing there would be another event inside, so he has asked me to fetch you, Sir, and to take you to an alternative venue."

He stared at me, bewildered. I began to wonder whether I was going to have to revert to choking the bastard. "I'm not going anywhere with you," the Major blurted.

"All I can do is explain to you what's going on, Sir. The gentleman from the Lords, who I now provide security for, was due to meet you here. He got in touch with you, in the hope of engaging you to provide a service for him. Because of the phone tapping situation, he needed to say that it was in relation to an innocuous matter, and I suggested that because of our past," I gestured between us, "he should tell you that it concerned me. Two birds as it were. Belfast, and a colleague whom you dismissed, Sir."

The Major grunted in disapproval.

"If you would follow me Sir, the gentleman would like to talk to you at a different location, because of the media presence at this one."

He regarded me with deep suspicion, but I didn't want to give him any more thinking time, so I turned on my heel and began walking. In his bafflement, he followed. Not a word was spoken. I was the servant, he the master. He remained at my heel as I turned down the wide entry, past the pub, and led him to the door of a church. There was a cold but decent-sized porch, dark and tiled. I stepped into the gloom and stood aside, waiting for his steps to fall in beside mine. He stood, looking at the Marian devotion, and decided he'd had enough. Peace process or no peace process, a Catholic Church in Belfast was no place for a British Naval Officer. The Major fumbled in his pocket for a mobile phone, and I struck him then, full force, in the Adam's apple.

It would take at least three minutes, probably more. This was a man with diver's lungs, fit as a trout. His arms flung me aside, and we battled for thirty seconds in that tiny porch, tight, close blows, aiming for the soft bits as we had been trained to do. Amateurs fight hard, knuckles on skulls, busted hands and eye sockets. Professionals fight dirty, gouging eyes, ripping bollocks, disabling quickly, cutting off air, vision, sound, touch.

The major didn't stand a chance. His airway was blocked and the energy only hastened his suffocation. I caught him as his knees gave way, gripping his shoulder and hugging him in tight. There were half a dozen people scattered throughout the vacuous, beautiful Church, as I manoeuvred him through the door. None of the worshippers looked around as I placed him at one of the rearmost pews, on his knees, head forward in prayer. No one disturbs the devout. He could be there for hours before anyone thought to check. I liberated his phone and wallet to further delay any identification, and left to meet his lunch date.

*****

He was lurking behind the floppy pages of the Daily Telegraph. A waist-coated waiter had showed me to his seat. All I had required was his name, with title, naturally. When the Brit saw me, his jaw dropped with the broad pages of the paper, but he did his best to gain composure.

"M'lud," I said, sitting in the armchair opposite, and drawing it in close. "The Major regrets that he will not be able to join you for luncheon," I said, overly sarcastic, on reflection. But I had just killed a man, and everything becomes a little dramatic in such circumstances. The Brit stared at me. I drew out my new phone, stroked it to life, and fired up a video the twin had placed on its memory. Then I leaned in, so that he could hear it, and turned the screen towards him.

It was natural that he should pitch forward, conspiratorially, afraid of being overheard. I tapped the little arrow to begin the entertainment.

"Look you little Belgian bastard," it began. He watched himself on a split screen for less than two seconds, before he closed his eyes, and fell back into his chair. His head tilted back, and his neck arched to the ceiling. His eyes re-opened, and he stared at the beams above him.

"They're all there," I said, wagging the phone at him. "We've even got my meeting with the professor in New York. The Keeper is gone, but you probably know that by now."

His flinched, for the first time. That was evidently news to him. I waited. Eventually he spoke, softly. "People like you will never understand, that there are times when things like this are required, in order to bring about a better outcome for everyone." His delivery was slow, almost sad.

"Is this where you tell me that your rape and abuse are justified for the greater good?" I asked.

"Oh, I'm not an abuser. I never was. I simply pulled the strings, you see."

His tone was pompous, as if he were explaining a complicated principle to a dunce. I listened. There was much I still didn't know.

"That way we can get people to move in the correct direction, towards peace perhaps, or persuade influential figures to do the right thing. You see, the public doesn't always vote for what is good for them. They are emotional, they are volatile, they give in to their urges, their angers, their fears. You know all about that, don't you Sam? You know what it is to give in to violence, to allow your impulses to take over."

I ignored the goading. "So, your Circle of abuse is the fault of the general public, for voting for the wrong people?" My tone was incredulous.

He sighed, as if I were more to be pitied than scolded. "I was responsible for delivering certain things, certain outcomes. I had to achieve my targets, just like anyone else. In my line, things were left to me to determine. How I achieved those ends was left largely up to me."

"And your target was?"

"To make important people compliant, of course. If you compromise somebody, in a salacious way, then you have that chap at your mercy. This is not a new concept Sam, it was always thus."

"So 'the Heir' was skinned, and raped, and imprisoned, to what end?"

"Well, peace in Ireland was achieved many ways Sam, and every element contributed. There was your lot of course, the military and what have you. There was influence, from America and elsewhere. But there was also a certain amount of manipulation, in order to get the politicians to do what was required, to change their minds, their positions on certain matters. Politicians in Northern Ireland are particularly belligerent, as you know, so we required what the Americans might call 'leverage,' pressure, persuasion. The truth is that the Heir was being abused long before we ever came across the Visitors, and their ghastly little circle."

Visitors. Visiting. The Professor's computer password suddenly made sense.

I shook my head. "But you led the Visitors," I said, "that's clear from all of the recordings."

"Ultimately, perhaps, but not the abuse. I rather insinuated control, which is removed from participation. It took quite some time, Sam, years as a matter of fact, but I assure you, the results were really very pleasing."

The riddles irritated me. "So, you came across the abuse group, and somehow joined it, and then became the boss, in order to blackmail its members to bring about peace?"

"As part of the effort," he shrugged, as if he were proud but humble to have done his bit.

"That means you allowed the rape and abuse to continue, when you could have stopped it," I said.

"You're not appreciating the complexity of this Sam, really. This was just one string to very broad bow. You have rather got in the way. You've served your country well, but you're an oily rag. You'll never understand those who serve in more intelligent ways."

"I don't think the Guardian newspaper, or the New York Times will understand it either, when they receive these videos," I said.

"No doubt they're ready to go, from your friend's twin sister, or that money-grabbing little foreigner," he said. "But it is of little consequence now."

And with that, he reached forward and popped a pill into his glass of white wine. Panic seized me, as I anticipated the arrival of others to pin me back and force it down my throat. He read me like a book.

"Oh no Sam, this is not for you. I'm aware that I've made a few faux pas, as it were. Allowing myself to be recorded was a touch of naivety from an old dog in a new world. I often wonder why we go to such lengths to gain access to encrypted media, when in fact, a twelve-year-old can work out how to record it, as if setting a tape for the Antiques Roadshow."

"Who do you work for?" I asked.

"Nobody. Anymore. But there are always loose ends when one has dabbled in the things I've been involved in. Few are quite as convoluted as this. Nonetheless, I had hoped to tidy up and end my retirement in the Lords. You've become a spoke in the works."

"How do you manage? To carry on, when you know there are children being raped like that?"

"Bit rich, is it not Sam? You carry on with your extra-judicial existence. How many people have you dispatched in the past year?"

I didn't really want to start counting, to be honest.

"Of course, you're quite right. The shame for me," he shook his head, "too much. Much too much." He drank back the golden fluid. "Rather unpleasant drop, that," he looked at his glass, "to finish with, which is a shame."

I looked into his eyes for a hint of what was to come. "I don't expect compassion from a brute like you," he said, "but if there were any means by which I could be kept out of the picture, it would rather serve you well."

I almost laughed at him.

"I intend to stop these "Visitors," this ring, this Circle," I told him.

"Yes, I quite follow. If you are prepared to do that without going to the newspapers, I shall agree to help you. But it will require a gentleman's agreement, and time is tight."

I snorted at him. "Are you for real?"

"Quite real, as you put it, Sam. Now, if you deal with these people without exposing this whole saga, I shall entrust to you the job I had intended to pass to your former boss, the Major."

"What?"

"I shall give you the information you will require to close down the Circle. Of course, I had intended that the Major see to you as well, but that plan has rather gone awry."

I stared at him, utterly incredulous. "You wanted the major to kill me, and then the members of the Circle?"

"Exactly," he said. "You see, the Major is not entirely squeaky clean either, and as you have proven so difficult to contain, I rather imagined it would take someone with similar skills to yours, but perhaps better breeding and intelligence, to snuff you out."

"And this is supposed to persuade me to protect you?"

"Not me, Sam, I am done for. As I say, time is tight. In fact, you have just moments to make your mind up. Agree to deal with these people quietly, and live with your child in blissful abandon upon the ocean wave."

"Or what?"

"Or forever look over your shoulder. You see Sam, you're not the only one with contingencies."

I shook my head in utter bewilderment. He pressed on. "I need an answer, now."

"Ok," I said. He nodded, and took out his own phone, selected a contact, and spoke.

"You can stand down, no further action is necessary on the continent, understood?"

I couldn't hear the answer, but I could hear that there was someone on the other end of the call. Then the Brit reached around his back. I tensed to pounce. He was astonishingly calm.

"It's ok, Sam," he said in his consistently condescending tone, "it's merely a gift." He handed me a folder of light cardboard, as if it had been taken from an old filing cabinet. The tab on the top was handwritten. "VISITORS," it said.

Within minutes, the Brit was shaking, whatever he'd swallowed was making its mark. "They'll all go quietly, just like me, if you manage it correctly."

His final words, before the induced stroke erupted inside his head.

*****

I lifted his wine glass and dropped it into the cardboard folder. He looked as if he was asleep. I imagined such a state was not uncommon in clubs like that, so I walked gently out, noting the absence of CCTV cameras. With my hat on my head, I took some comfort from the fact that anyone inquiring after his lunch companion would consult the guest list, and then search for someone else. A Major in the Royal Navy no less, who was in fact dead in a nearby Church. All of that would pose quite a conundrum for any investigator, but by the time they worked it all out, if ever, I would be well offshore.

I didn't open the file until I got back to the boat. Inside were the images and profiles of a dozen people. Taped to a piece of paper was a tiny computer memory drive, smaller than an SD card. Beside it was a scrawl.

"All sorts of compromising behaviour there, enough to achieve the goal." A note from some sort of establishment-sponsored manipulator, to my former Major. Now my responsibility.

There was an A4 sheet with twelve photos. I gave it a glance. At least two were influential figures in Irish politics, back-roomers, the powerful ones. They were the type who had the clout to manipulate big decisions. I presumed the Brit had used his leverage to employ them to do his bidding. I'd heard enough about the brutality involved to give the rest of the file a miss, for now. I already knew what I would do with the information, but that could wait.

Notions of sending the videos to the press vanished. I felt, for the first time, that Isla and I had an opportunity. I feared becoming drawn in, of having our privacy compromised, of disrupting the peace I needed to build around her.

I peeled out of my suit, and layered up for a long haul. The windlass ground the anchor aboard, the donkey fired and the impeller hove water in to cool the engine. I set the autohelm and skipped on deck to unleash the sails. Then I sat at the navigation table and pulled out the almanac for information on the tides heading south. Biscay, Lisbon, Gibraltar, Valencia I reckoned. If I didn't stop, and with good breeze, I might make it in eight days.

*****

I never asked what was on the memory card. The twin made copies, the Belgian tracked down the addresses. Each was posted a copy of their compromising behaviour. I read the obituaries in the online sections of newspapers. Ten of the Circle, the *Visitors* as they called themselves, perished at their own instigation. The Keeper made eleven, which left one. For the time being, I chose to let him worry, and run.

The Charity woman dealt with the Heir. That poor woman's location had formed the Keeper's last sentence. I passed it to Charity, outlined her circumstances, and didn't ask any more. I knew the victim was in good hands. I had others to care for.

I picked them up in a small marina, in a town called Palamos, on the east coast of Spain. Dad wasn't Olympic, but for a seventy-something with a freshly punctured lung, he was in astonishing shape.

Isla was brilliant, just brilliant. Her little arms wrapped around my neck and we hugged for ten solid minutes before I swung her aboard, and gave her her orders. Like the salty little seabird she'd become, she fell into line, busying herself with the warps, as my mum and dad looked on with pride. Brown as a berry and steady as a rock, she leaned into me as the breeze took the cutter and healed her to lee. With the warm breeze on our necks and a glass in our paws, we left the coast of one country, and headed to another.

ABOUT FINN

Finn Óg is a pseudonym. "Charlie" is his first book. Finn lives and works in Ireland, is surrounded by rogues and does not venture inland unless absolutely necessary. To find out more or to be among the first to get the next book in the series (when it's finished) please visit:

www.finnog.com

A taster from the second part in the trilogy...

CHARLIE II
THE CROSSING

The world is irritatingly small.

Sam stood on Dublin's Grafton Street, watched the man go up in flames, and cursed how approximate people have become. He sighed, for a moment, and watched the crowd part like a sea of red, the glow of the inferno flickering off their faces, horrifying and beguiling in almost equal measure. He shook his head, looked to the sky, and then stepped forward to douse the screams. He would grow to wish he'd let the man burn.

**

"Snap!"

Isla was cheating, as usual, in part due to a misunderstanding of the rules. At six years old, the fun was more in beating her father to the claim, than in stockpiling cards, and so she shouted before the face had been flipped. It gave Sam delight too, to watch how her little mind anticipated his hand movements, to see her excitement. It seemed like a normal, wholesome thing to do of an evening, after all that the wee woman had been through.

They were drifting, alone, across the Mediterranean, in their fifty-four foot home. It was deliberately slow progress, there had been a lot of re-building to do, and the work was far from finished. Sam doubted whether his daughter's scars would ever properly heal, but she was gradually becoming less afraid of bedtime, and of the potential horror that sleep could bring her.

He'd made resolutions, starting with work. He wouldn't take on any job that could possibly impact upon his daughter, or his family. The last assignment he'd become embroiled in had done that and more, and nearly killed his father. From here on in Sam determined, any risks taken would be his alone, and even at that, they would be minimal. He had a child to raise, and she had no mother to step into the breach.

"Daddy you can have some of my cards," Isla told him, sliding a frugal collection to his side of the chart table.

"Thank you darlin'," said Sam, the salt and the stubble tautening at a gentle reminder of his daughter's provenance. Isla's mother would never see anyone stuck, winning had never been Finn's priority. "What story do you want tonight?"

"Aw-uh, is it bedtime already?"

"Not yet little lady, but in a while."

It had become part of the ritual, to keep the imagery gentle. Stories at night, of normal life, of other girls, of school and excitement and toys and boys and the weird and horrible things they do. Sam's plan was to encourage Isla to want such things again, to grow the appeal of ordinariness, rather than the nomadic sea-gypsy style they had become accustomed to. Although the perpetual sailing suited Sam, and for a while had seemed to be the best way to make Isla feel safe, the time would come when she would have to swim in the real world again. So their grift, when the wind blew them west, was aimed at Ireland once more.

By night Sam plotted the charts, and the future, and occasionally sailed. It allowed Isla to keep watch while he dozed by day in the cockpit. She had become quite the little sailor; she was careful and clipped on at all times above deck, and he trusted her. Mostly, they anchored or found a marina at night, but occasionally, when the notion took him, he would stand at the helm and allow his own healing. The breeze would peel back his grief, and the anonymity and privacy of the sea would allow him to let the stream roll down his cheeks. Such moments kept his pain from Isla, avoiding her interrogation and worry. He would never allow her to see him weep. She understood how much he missed his wife, her mother, but it would never be the same as it was for her. Isla had not just lost her mam, she had seen her die. They had spoken as she bled out. Isla had held her hand and looked into the face of her killer, convinced that she would be next. And worse still, she had believed that it was all her fault.

Sam read to her until the rise and ebb of her little body slowed, and he curled his neck to make sure she was deep enough to extract his arm from under her. Then he paused, for ten minutes, watching her eyelids for any sign of disturbance. Placated, he went on deck and indulged his maudlin currents, allowing himself to be swept back to better times, and to lament his loss. That's when the tears came. Eventually he would snap out of it and start to sail the boat properly, but for a while, he would purge. It brought an odd sort of pleasure, the wallowing, the reminiscence.

He was shaken by Isla's little face appearing in the companionway, the yellow light breaking his night vision as she came up the steps.

"What was that Daddy?" she said.

"What wee lamb?" Sam replied, scraping the tears from the crevices in his face.

"The noise, the whistle."

Sam turned his ears from the wind and stood stock still, but could catch nothing.

"There, can you hear it daddy?"

"No love, I think you better go back to sleep," he said, pressing the autohelm and checking the radar screen to make sure their course was clear.

He was lifting her into her bunk when she said it again.

"There it is daddy, why can't you hear that?"

"You're dreaming wee love, you're still a bit asleep," he told her, tucking her in, keen to get back to the helm in case of any debris in the sea.

"I'm not daddy, I'm really, really not," she replied.

"Ok, I'll go up and keep an ear out," he said, as he hugged her. He was worried that she might not sleep now, and was anxious that they were sailing with no watch above. "I love you so much," he said, and returned to the cockpit.

And then came the sound, high-pitched, audible to younger ears at a distance, older ones when up close. And it was close. Amid one hundred thousand square miles of sea, Sam and Isla were no longer alone, and every resolution he had made, went over the side.

Printed in Great Britain
by Amazon